ALL HALLOWS' EVE

OTHER BOOKS BY VIVIAN VANDE VELDE

Remembering Raquel

Three Good Deeds

The Book of Mordred

Now You See It . . .

Wizard at Work

Heir Apparent

Being Dead

Magic Can Be Murder

Alison, Who Went Away

The Rumpelstiltskin Problem

There's a Dead Person Following My Sister Around

Never Trust a Dead Man

A Coming Evil

Smart Dog

Curses, Inc., and Other Stories

Tales from the Brothers Grimm and the Sisters Weird

Companions of the Night

Dragon's Bait

User Unfriendly

A Well-Timed Enchantment

A Hidden Magic

Vivian Vande Velde

ALL HALLOWS' EVE

13 stories

Houghton Mifflin Harcourt

Boston   New York

The text of this book is set in Bembo.

Library of Congress Cataloging-in-Publication Data
Vande Velde, Vivian.
All Hallows' Eve: 13 stories / Vivian Vande Velde.
p. cm.
Summary: Presents thirteen tales of Halloween horrors, including ghosts,
vampires, and pranks gone awry.
ISBN 978-0-15-205576-9 hardcover
ISBN 978-0-15-206473-0 paperback
1. Halloween—Juvenile fiction. 2. Supernatural—Juvenile fiction. 3. Children's stories,
American. [1. Halloween—Fiction. 2. Supernatural—Fiction. 3. Horror stories.
4. Short stories.]
I. Title
PZ7.V2773A11 2006
[Fic]—dc22 2006005439

Manufactured in the United States of America

DOH 10 9 8 7 6 5 4

4500552269

Contents

Come in and Rest a Spell
1

MARIAN
9

Morgan Roehmar's Boys
29

Only on All Hallows' Eve
61

Cemetery Field Trip
71

Best Friends

97

Pretending

111

I Want to Thank You

137

When and How

141

When My Parents Come to Visit

155

Edward, Lost and Far from Home

175

My Real Mother

189

Holding On

215

To the members of RACWI
(Rochester Area Children's
Writers & Illustrators),
whose support is legendary

ALL HALLOWS' EVE

COME IN AND REST
A SPELL

Don't be shy. Don't be afraid. Come on in. Granny doesn't bite. See, Granny has hardly any teeth left. I couldn't bite if I wanted to.

Are you nervous because it's All Hallows' Eve? This *is* a spooky night. The dead walk, witches convene, a door opens between the world of the seen and the world of the unseen.

And sometimes that door lets all sorts of evil onto the earth.

No, no, don't leave. I'm just telling stories. Silly old granny that I am. The night is cold and dark, and you've walked so far to get here, and I just want to help you.

Eye of newt
Mandrake root
Tear of pity from a heartless soul . . .

Granny is good at helping people. No one has ever complained.

Let me guess what you need.

You're such a pretty young thing, with skin so soft and smooth, and your hair thick and dark, and your eyes clear, and your limbs firm and strong, and you even have all your teeth. Lucky, lucky you.

Granny misses her teeth.

What could a girl like you possibly need? What keeps you from being happy?

Is there sickness in your family? No, no, don't answer: Granny is guessing. And Granny would have guessed, even before you shook your head, that you don't have the look of someone dealing with that particular sorrow.

Are you needing money to survive? No, you're too beautiful to have done without meals or to be having no place to lay your head at night.

Is there someone who has crossed you, someone you want to put a curse on? Maybe . . . but Granny thinks you probably know how to get back at people, so you wouldn't need magic for that.

Granny guesses she sees a light in your eyes—not fever, or hunger, or the thought of revenge.

Granny guesses it's love. Granny guesses you're in love with a boy who doesn't love you back.

See! Granny's good at this.

Granny can help.

Wing of bat
Tooth of rat
Water that someone has drowned in . . .

Is he handsome? Is he rich?

Oh, yes, Granny knows the young man you mean. Granny thinks he's a fine choice. If Granny were younger, she'd want him for herself.

Granny has just the spell to bind him to you.

Granny must mix this, and this, and a little bit of this.

Yes, yes, it smells bad, but it's just what you need.

Drink it all.

All.

Yes, every last bit.

He will love your face, and your form, and your voice, and the way you move.

To be happy, he will need to see your eyes, to hear your laugh, to smell your scent, to touch your skin, to taste your lips. To be happy, he will need your happiness.

He will find completeness only in you.

Stain of blood
Graveyard mud
Dying breath of a murdered man . . .

5

You may feel light-headed.

Oops, Granny warned you. Here, take my hands. Granny will hold you steady while the spell works its way through you.

Yes, you're perfectly right: *He* needs to drink down the potion that will tie him to you.

Or should I say: to your beautiful, healthy, young body.

I'll make sure he drinks that.

The spell I just did? That lets us trade, you and Granny.

Don't struggle. It's no use, and you'll only bruise our beautiful skin.

Do you feel your limbs growing sore and weak? Do you recognize your features forming on me?

It's no use screaming; Granny is the only one who can hear.

Fine, then. Be that way: Let go of my hands. Too late now, anyway.

Oh, Granny sees. You're not so much recoiling from me as convulsing from the poison.

Did I forget to mention the poison?

I can't very well have you complaining about me. Granny has never had any complaints.

You just go ahead and lie there on the floor. It

won't be too much longer, and the pain won't get much worse.

I'll go see to your young man.

He and I will be very happy together.

And if we're not—I have a spell for that, too.

MARIAN

Justin saw the sign that said SPEED LIMIT: 8 MPH, and he saw the sign that said SPEED BUMP. But he wasn't a wimp, so he didn't slow down.

He didn't know why they even bothered putting numbers lower than twenty on the speedometer, anyway. There was driving, and there was parking, and as far as Justin was concerned, thirty miles per hour was the cutoff between the two. Even in an apartment complex, there was no need for such exaggerated care. They should give people credit: Anyone backing out of a parking space would know enough to look before pulling into the lane; and yeah, yeah, sure there were kids—there were enough signs warning KIDS AT PLAY—but any kid who lived in an apartment complex grew up knowing you play on the grass, not the pavement.

Besides, it was past eleven o'clock at night. Even on Halloween, that was later than the time kids should be out roaming and looking for opportunities to dart in front of cars.

Besides all that, Justin figured he was a better-than-average driver, and—as opposed to, for example, his parents' generation—his reflexes were honed by years of playing computer games.

And on top of everything else, adding bumps to a driving surface seemed not only counterintuitive but an affront to a civilized society.

So when he saw the SPEED BUMP sign, he figured he could slow down to a crawl and ease his car over it—*thump, thump,* front wheels; *thump, thump,* back wheels—or he could hit it fast enough that his car would momentarily become airborne and sail right over the obstruction in one smooth move.

He'd perfected this technique at his own apartment complex. But this night he'd been visiting Andrea—whose party had turned out to be as lame as kindergarten once her parents had come home earlier than expected from helping Grandma hand out Halloween goodies in *her* building. The speed bumps in this complex were taller, or wider, or steeper, or *something different* from what he was used to.

His car went up, then bottomed out with a force that he felt all the way up his spine and into his teeth.

The car was secondhand—or more likely third- or fourth- or fifth-hand—and had lousy springs.

One of the warning lights flickered—CHECK ENGINE, DOOR AJAR, FASTEN SEATBELTS—it was gone too fast to know which it had been. And something seemed to have rattled loose in the dashboard. There was a noise like static, as though the radio were coming on between stations.

This didn't seem likely, as the radio hadn't worked since September—since about five minutes after Justin gave the guy the money for the car. You knew you were pathetic when you bought a car a college kid was dumping. But Justin turned the volume dial up, anyway.

A sexy female voice said, "This is MARIAN: Mobile And Regional Interactive Assisted Navigation. How may I help you?"

Justin took his hand away from the radio dial so he could turn the steering wheel as he pulled out of Andrea's apartment complex and onto the street. He expected that whatever radio program he'd happened upon—the law of probability indicated it would be a commercial—would continue.

But it didn't.

The face of the radio wasn't lit up, and he wondered if two wires had made momentary contact during the jostling, only to disconnect again.

Still, Justin was an optimist, and he turned the

volume knob up a bit higher, then he changed the station to see if anything came in.

Slightly louder, the voice repeated, "This is MARIAN: Mobile And Regional Interactive Assisted Navigation. How may I help you?"

The most logical explanation was *still* a commercial. Just his luck to get the same commercial on two different stations. But Justin repeated—softly, even though there was no one to hear him making a fool of himself—"MARIAN?"

The voice asked, "What is your destination?"

Feeling like an idiot, Justin again said, "MARIAN?"

The voice said, "Mobile And Regional Interactive Assisted Navigation."

Just when it seemed the conversation was doomed to go in circles forever, the voice added, "This system is similar to a GPS, but with higher interactive capability."

A voice-activated Global Positioning System. The college kid certainly had not said anything about a built-in GPS. He *had* pointed out there was a CD player, without mentioning it was so motion-sensitive it was useless. There was air-conditioning, but it took about an hour and a half to cool the car down. Obviously the GPS had stopped working—a loose something-or-other, which the speed bump had repositioned.

But it probably still didn't work *properly*—that would be too much to ask for. "MARIAN, huh?" Justin asked. Still not believing, he went on, "If you're so smart, where am I?"

The voice—MARIAN—enunciated each word distinctly but didn't have a synthesized sound to it at all—more like a slightly prissy English teacher than a mechanical device. She— It— It was hard to know *how* to think of the thing. She said, "You are in the town of Waverly in the county of Lancaster in New York State. You are traveling sixty-seven miles per hour going eastbound on Church Street between Cricket Hill Lane and Ferguson Road. Would you like your latitude and longitude?"

Justin let up on the gas to slow down just enough to read the oncoming street sign.

"Sixty-six miles per hour," the voice amended, "sixty-five, sixty-four . . ."

Sure enough, when he saw the sign, it said FERGU-SON RD.

The GPS may not have been working before, but it sure was working now.

"Naw," Justin said. "No latitude and longitude. And you don't need to keep telling me my speed—you sound like my mother."

"The MARIAN system does not mean to criticize your driving. The MARIAN system was simply reporting statistics."

It was a good thing the college kid who'd sold him the car hadn't known the GPS was so easily fixed or he would have charged even more. As the car had almost a hundred thousand miles on it, Justin already felt he had been overcharged. One fender was primer gray and the rest of the car was dull blue dotted by rust. Maybe the guy hadn't even known about the GPS. It wasn't like there was obvious equipment, like Justin's uncle Herm needed to set on the dashboard of *his* car. Just this sexy voice coming out of his radio speaker.

"Okay, MARIAN," Justin said, "how about you tell me the best way to get home from here?" Not that he needed a GPS for that.

"Please state your home address," MARIAN said, "and define 'best' as 'most scenic,' 'shortest distance,' or 'quickest time.'"

"Three seventy-six Buggy Whip Lane," Justin said, "in Baldwin. And *of course* 'best' means 'fastest.'"

"Calculating route," MARIAN told him.

A moment later the voice resumed: "Normally, the fastest route would be via the 790 expressway, but there is an accident in the eastbound lane 4.3 miles beyond the Jefferson Avenue access road."

"How do you know that?" Justin asked.

"From monitoring police-band frequencies. A gasoline tanker has overturned and is leaking, so traffic is being detoured off the expressway at Jefferson Avenue, then being routed through the town of Hadleyport and sent via Goose Hill Road to Route 37 in Craigmont. Unfortunately, the satellite feed shows there are construction delays on Route 37 due to a repaving crew working from 7:00 P.M. to 4:00 A.M., but—"

"Never mind," Justin said. Even this late at night when the traffic wouldn't be too heavy, he didn't want to do that. It was a good thing MARIAN had turned on when she had. "What do you recommend?"

"Recalculating," MARIAN said.

Then she said, "You can avoid the expressway entirely by turning right at the next intersection, Pinnacle Road. Estimated time of arrival at 376 Buggy Whip Lane is 11:42 P.M., eastern time, twenty-five minutes, twenty-six seconds. Pinnacle Road intersection approaching in 2.66 miles, approximately two minutes, twenty-five seconds away—estimations made at your current speed of sixty-six miles per hour. The speed limit on this stretch of Church Street is posted at fifty-five miles per hour."

"Yes, Mother," Justin grumbled.

"A speeding ticket that indicates a speed of eleven

miles per hour over the posted limit would range in cost—"

"You aren't going to turn me in, are you?" Justin whipped his foot off the accelerator. That would be worse than being caught by radar—having his own vehicle report him to the police.

But MARIAN said, "The MARIAN system can listen in on the bands used by emergency vehicles but will not contact them except when the driver directs me to, or when catastrophic system failure of the car has occurred, indicating an accident."

"Okay," Justin said, putting his foot back on the accelerator. He made the right-hand turn onto Pinnacle Road with a screech of tires. Perhaps slowing down a bit might not have been a totally bad idea.

"You are now traveling southbound on Pinnacle Road. Recalculating. Estimated time of arrival to 376 Buggy Whip Lane, twenty-two minutes, forty seconds. Next turn will be in 5.8 miles—a left-hand turn, eastbound, onto Lincoln Road/Route 81."

"This is great!" Justin said. He slowed down or speeded up simply to hear MARIAN say, "Recalculating."

"Would you like to utilize the points-of-interest function?" MARIAN offered.

"We're in the town of Waverly," Justin said. "There *are* no points of interest."

"You have crossed the border into the town of Stewart," MARIAN corrected him.

"Whatever. All I see is farms."

"Gus's Auto Transmission and Fresh Vegetable Mart is on the left-hand side of the road in another 167 yards."

Sure enough, they passed Gus's, though, being almost eleven thirty at night, the place was closed—much good it would have done him, even if he had been looking for it. The chalkboard sign in front of the place advertised: HALLOWEEN SPECIAL—PUMPKINS 75% OFF.

Just to see what would happen, he intentionally drove past Lincoln Road, even though MARIAN reminded him of the turn at five hundred feet away. She then said, "Off route. Recalculating." Rather than telling him to stop the car and turn around, she figured out a new route from the point where he currently was.

A few more turns, and Justin had absolutely no idea where they were, but that was okay since MARIAN obviously knew *exactly*.

And then, suddenly, out there in the middle of nowhere, the engine stopped and the car coasted to a standstill.

Justin checked the gas gauge, but it indicated he still had a little more than a quarter of a tank.

"What's up?" he asked.

MARIAN was just a GPS, but she was so interactive—so personable—he was not surprised when she turned out to be an engine diagnostician, too.

"Vapor lock," she said.

"'Vapor lock'?" Justin repeated. "While I was moving?"

"Coupled with bad antifreeze."

"'Bad antifreeze'?"

"Turn the key to off," MARIAN said. "Wait five minutes, then turn the key in the ignition *without* pumping the accelerator. Recalculating. Estimated time of arrival to 376 Buggy Whip Lane, fourteen minutes, three seconds."

Justin muttered that he'd never heard of such a thing, but he did as MARIAN instructed.

The fall night was perfectly quiet.

Justin tried humming, but he couldn't carry a tune, and he sounded bad even to himself. He had asked his parents for a new CD player for the car for Christmas, but he didn't think he'd be able to wait two months.

MARIAN announced: "Four more minutes till you can turn the engine back on."

"Hey," Justin said. "How come you're still working when the engine is turned off?"

"Backup generator."

"Can the backup generator keep the heat on?"

"No," MARIAN said.

Not that the heat worked much better than the air conditioner.

Justin leaned back in the seat and looked around.

This was when he noticed that his car was sitting directly on some railroad tracks.

"Ahmm, MARIAN," he said, "did you happen to notice where we've stalled?"

MARIAN said, "CFX line on the Syracuse to Buffalo route."

"But," Justin said hopefully, "not currently in use?"

MARIAN said, "Three more minutes till you can turn the engine back on."

Justin tried again. He asked, "Is this, like, one of those abandoned railroad lines?"

"No," MARIAN said.

And just as she said it, Justin heard, in the distance—but not-too-great distance—the wail of a train whistle.

There was also a bell.

A mechanical arm lowered and came to rest on the roof of Justin's car.

MARIAN told him, "The next train is scheduled to pass this spot in two minutes, twenty-seven seconds."

Justin hurriedly leaned forward to turn the key in the ignition.

MARIAN warned, "If you turn the key, you will delay the release of the vapor lock for another five minutes, and the train will pass here in two minutes, fourteen seconds."

"But," Justin said, "but—"

"Two more minutes till you can turn the engine back on. That will give you twelve seconds to start the car and drive it off the tracks."

"Twelve seconds?" Justin couldn't get his voice above a whisper. "That's cutting it awfully close." He looked to his left and thought he could see the light from the oncoming train. "Surely it doesn't need to be exactly five minutes for me to turn the car back on—"

"Five minutes total," MARIAN told him firmly. "From now: one minute, fifty-four seconds till you can turn the engine back on and be certain the vapor lock is gone."

And what if the vapor lock *wasn't* gone? What if the engine didn't start on its first try? Justin asked, "How sure are you about that train? If you're off by just a couple seconds—"

"Monitoring by satellite feed. At current speed, the train will arrive at this spot in one minute, fifty-one seconds. New York State regulations stipulate a train should reduce speed when approaching an intersection, so in theory you will have even more than twelve seconds."

The train's headlights shone in the distance. The whistle sounded again. Would the engineer be able to make out that there was an obstruction on the tracks? Justin's hand itched to turn the key. Could there really be that big a difference between waiting the full five minutes and waiting only four and a half minutes?

Twelve seconds. Twelve seconds to start the engine and to get the car off the tracks.

And if—for some reason—the car didn't start right away, he'd have time to try, maybe, once more. Twelve seconds to watch the train crashing into him. Twelve seconds to die.

"One more minute till you can turn the engine back on," MARIAN announced.

The train's whistle was blowing frantically—surely a sign that the engineer had spotted him.

"The train is decelerating," MARIAN said, and sure enough Justin could hear the screech of brakes. "Fifty seconds till you can turn the engine back on; sixty-seven seconds till the train reaches this spot."

Justin knew that a train could not stop quickly. The more cars the engine was pulling, the more time the train would need to come to a standstill. Justin couldn't take it any longer. He fumbled for his seat belt.

MARIAN said, "Don't panic. There is enough time to restart your engine and to drive to safety."

Justin yanked on the door handle but got caught in the seat belt, which hadn't had time to retract fully yet.

MARIAN said, "If you leave the car, the train will collide with it, and your vehicle will be destroyed. Thirty-six seconds till you can turn the engine back on; fifty-five seconds till the train reaches this spot."

Justin disentangled himself from the seat belt and stumbled out of the car.

MARIAN said, "Outside of the vehicle, you are likely to be injured by flying debris. Return to the car. You may now restart your engine."

She'd just said thirty-six seconds, and all of a sudden she was saying he could do it now.

MARIAN said, "The train is fifty seconds away. Return to the car."

She was lying. In horror, Justin realized she was lying. She wanted him to get back in the car so he could drive off the tracks—even though that would put him in danger. She was saying it because there was no way for *her* to leave the car.

For *it* to leave the car.

The GPS wanted him to risk his life so *it* wouldn't get damaged.

Tough luck, despite the sexy voice.

Justin began running.

Marian Bartholomeo let her consciousness seep out of the car radio, even though she could not be damaged by anything in the physical world.

She watched as the train smashed into the stalled car.

As she had predicted, pieces went flying. But the boy was far enough away that none of them hit him. That was okay. She would have liked to kill him, because he was a bad driver and a dangerous jerk, and it would have been a good deed to get him permanently off the streets, but he hadn't been her primary target. The train stayed on the track, which was fine with her—she didn't have anything against trains.

But she was delighted to see the wreckage of the car. For it had been this very car that had ended her life not two months ago.

Of course her first target had been the driver, that terrible college kid who had been drinking and driving and had not even known that he had run her over.

Already dead, she'd watched him wake up the following morning and waited for him to realize what he'd done. She waited for him to express his grief and remorse.

He saw the broken headlight, the dent in the fender, her blood on the bumper. She had thought he would cry out in anguish, beg forgiveness from her and from the heavens, and dedicate his life to good deeds in reparation.

Instead, he hosed the blood off, bought a replacement headlight, and placed an ad in the local paper to sell the car, to get rid of the evidence.

She had spent the last two months hounding him, whispering to him in his dreams, whispering to him when he was drinking. "Your fault," she had whispered. "Your fault, your fault, your fault."

She didn't know if it was the whispering or the drinking, but at the Halloween party his dorm was hosting tonight, he had tripped over the hem of his Phantom of the Opera costume cape, fallen down a set of stairs, and broken his neck.

That was when she'd gone after his car, and found it just as that other reckless boy was tearing through the apartment-complex parking lot—another driver looking for an accident to happen. She had used his hitting those speed bumps to make him think he'd jostled something loose in his dashboard.

So now, her task on Earth was finished.

Except . . .

It had been kind of fun pretending to be a GPS.

Maybe, she thought, she'd find another bad teenage driver.

Or two.

Or three.

MORGAN ROEHMAR'S BOYS

Ashley rearranged the dead bodies, because there's nothing worse than a messy dead body.

Witches, people could recognize by the cackling laughter; werewolves growled and lunged; and vampires swooped. All of those induced honestly earned alarm. But dead bodies just lay or sit there like so much bloodstained laundry, and if people couldn't tell this was a scene of mass murder and were only startled by the light coming on, what was the point of that?

Ashley centered the pitchfork, which had a tendency to sag, in the chest of the man tied to the chair, and she fluffed the hair of the severed head, making sure the executioner's ax was perpendicular against the neck of the torso a yard or so away, so that the woman's decapitation looked recent, not like tired, old news.

"Barn ready," she said into the microphone of her headset. She took the time to make sure the hanged man—who had a tendency to rotate at the end of his rope—had his face turned toward the door for best effect. She had as much time as she needed between wagonloads, within reason, for the drivers slowed their tractors by the hedgerow, waiting for her all clear. This ensured she had the light off before they turned the corner, even though the dim red light, enough for her to set up by, was not likely to be glimpsed from among the orchard's trees. Once she gave the okay, she had about thirty seconds to turn off the light before the tractor would circle around and be facing the barn; but she had another two minutes to settle herself before the tractor, pulling the hay wagon, would actually drive in through the open doors. At that point she would flick on the regular light, which was still dim to maximize spookiness.

She heard Tim's voice through the earpiece: "Okay, now, arms and legs inside the wagon; we don't want any injuries"—the "okay" being his signal that he had heard her and was on his way; the rest of what he said maybe necessary and maybe not for this particular wagonload of customers, but spoken to disguise his acknowledgment of her message.

Ashley lay down on her bale of hay, positioned beneath the murderer with the upraised knife. The hay smelled good but—packed tight—was hard and prickled like crazy. The front of her peasant dress was saturated with theatrical blood, and the customers would assume she was simply another mannequin in this tableau of death until—just as the wagon passed—she would jump up and fling herself at those riding on the back, screaming madly and making as though to grab them.

She pressed the top button on the remote control that turned off the red setup light, and took off her headset to hide it behind the bale of hay, where the customers wouldn't see it. The attached wire pulled the battery pack out of her pocket before she remembered to remove it, and it clunked to the floor. If she broke yet another one of those things, Nikko would throw a fit. In school he was quiet, never-having-a-contrary-opinion Nikko, and she had been *so* interested in him, even though he was a couple years older. But here he was the "family" part of Cristanis Family Farm, and his father let him run the haunted hayrides pretty much on his own, where he was an ogre—never mind that he didn't wear a costume. Ashley had just turned sixteen, and this was the first year she could work here, along with the seniors and college kids. Nikko may have turned out to be a disappointment, but it would be humiliating to get fired after only one week.

Ashley held the earpiece up to her ear and could hear the background noise of people squealing on one of the wagons, so she knew it still worked. Those performers who never got close to the customers, like the witches in the grotto, could pull the hair of their wigs over the headset and wear their wires more securely fastened beneath their costumes, but she—and the ghouls who chased the wagon—had to take the headset off at performance time.

As Ashley lay in the dark, she heard a rumble, which she would have assumed was the sound effects from Gina and Jordan doing their magic-cauldron act further up the trail, but it seemed to come from the wrong direction, more from the west, beyond the orchard.

Not thunder, she hoped. The weather forecast had said there was a possibility of storms, but that wasn't supposed to be till later, after closing. There were few enough days for the haunted hayrides. You couldn't have them in September: That was pushing the season and people weren't interested—or not enough to make it worthwhile being open; and you obviously had to stop after Halloween. It was a shame to lose nights to bad weather.

She had just convinced herself that she had imagined the rumble, when it came again. Closer this time. Definitely thunder. She could hear the tractor, too. She thought they'd come in—the thunder wasn't that close, but then, through the open doors, she saw a flicker of lightning. The lightning was diffuse—high up and far away—but she could hear the tractor swing around, even before she picked up the headset and heard Nikko announcing, "Tractors, return to the loading area. Tractors, back. We've got weather."

Of course, the tractors couldn't be out in the open fields during a thunderstorm where they'd be a sitting target for lightning, but the storm wasn't moving in that fast. Still, Nikko's father was a worrier, and that was one area of the operations Nikko had clear instructions about. Pulling the hay wagons in the cold was okay, even in the rain. But not during a storm.

Ashley heard Kat, in the witches' grotto, ask, "Should we come in?"

"Weather stations," Nikko told them, which meant he was hoping the storm was just skirting the area, so they were supposed to take shelter in the outbuildings but be prepared to start again. Nikko certainly wasn't going to be handing out refunds unless he had to.

Ashley reached for the remote control to get the light on and accidentally pressed the bottom button, the one that controlled both the light and the special effects.

A shuddering moan came from the speaker hidden in the hanged man.

The severed head winked.

The legs of the man tied to the chair jerked while the speaker in his body emitted pathetic sobs, which would eventually subside to whimpers, then a death gurgle—which nine out of ten people on the wagons never heard because *they* were too busy screaming in terror.

Ashley's knife-wielding murderer shouted, "Die, wench, die!" but only once before she cut the power.

This time she pressed the middle button on the remote control. There was only a single hundred-watt bulb for the whole barn, which provided the perfect balance of light and shadow for the show. It was enough to read a book by, at least for a little while, for those who were serious enough about their homework to bring it on the job with them just in case of unusual delays, but that certainly didn't include Ashley. It was enough light to play on a Gameboy, for anyone who had the foresight to bring one. Ashley lay back down on her bale of hay and did a few stomach crunches, but that got old fast, with the tight bodice of her peasant's dress instead of sweats.

There was a flash of lightning, distinct this time, and a roll of thunder only a few seconds later.

Nikko's tinny voice was coming through the earpiece, and Ashley picked it up from the floor and put it back on. He must have asked if everyone was secure, because people were counting off.

"Ashley, in the barn," she acknowledged when it

was her turn. She had hoped one or two of the ghouls—Ramon, if she'd had a choice, or even Karl—would have decided to take shelter in the barn, but they'd gone to the orchard shed, where there was a supply of cocoa, cider, apples, cheese, and doughnut holes. It's hard to compete for a teenage boy's attention when there's food involved.

"Shouldn't be long," Nikko assured them as Ashley, lying on her side, did vertical leg lifts. "Radar shows one area of disturbance just about directly overhead, but the rest is skimming off to the north. Just hang tight." That, despite the fact that the thunder was moving in much closer. Through the open door of the barn, Ashley got periodic glimpses of trees and sky as clear—for fractions of a second—as though it were full day.

"One Mississippi," someone counted off, "two—"

The thunder was no longer rumbling, but cracking.

"Hey, Ramon," she heard Dan ask—Dan, who, because he rode Riley as part of his Headless Horseman routine, got to wait out the storm in the Cristanis Farm's smaller barn, the one by the house—"how many vampires does it take to change a lightbulb?"

Ashley missed the answer due to static, which was probably from dropping her headset and/or the battery pack once too often. She jiggled the wire that connected them, and by then somebody else was off on a different joke—evidence, if she had needed it, that Dan's joke hadn't led to uncontrollable laughter.

"Here comes the rain," Nikko announced, and in another moment it started, as suddenly as someone turning on the shower, sharp and distinct-sounding, like an infinite number of thrown pebbles.

Ashley considered getting up to close the doors, but the rain was beating against the back of the barn, not blowing in.

Lightning flashed.

"One Mis—"

The thunder sounded like a tree breaking in half directly overhead.

"You doing okay, Ashley?" one of the Spagnola sisters asked—she couldn't tell whether it was Hannah or Lily.

"Sure," Ashley said, "nice and dry," thinking, *It couldn't have been one of the guys who asked?*

"Of all the places on this farm to be," Hannah or Lily started, but Nikko interrupted, "C'mon, girls."

"Just saying," whoever it was finished.

Ashley knew what that was all about: The sign out front might say CRISTANIS FAMILY FARM, but all these years later people still called it "the old Roehmar place." When Nikko's grandfather bought the place, in the seventies, it had sat empty for almost a decade because of the notoriety of what had happened there. He had the original house torn down—the house under whose floorboards the bodies of a half dozen boys and young men had been found. The bodies had been discovered when Morgan Roehmar, the original owner, had a lover's spat with his live-in woman friend. She told police about the occasional smell, which coincided with the disappearance of the high school cross-country runner in 1968, and the young Latino farmworker, who had supposedly never shown up in 1969.

Two generations of Cristanises lived in the new house, built on the opposite end of the property, and farmed the land. Two generations of Cristanises found it harder and harder to make ends meet.

Nikko's father had resisted the haunted-hayride idea, but the success enjoyed by several of the other farms in the area had persuaded him. He finally agreed, but had two rules:

- Avoid lawsuits.
- Don't cash in on real tragedy.

He forbade anything hinting at Morgan Roehmar and his obsession with good-looking boys, which was why the hayride's one dismembered body was a woman (Anne Boleyn, in case anyone asked), who'd lost her head to an ax, rather than a chain saw. And there definitely was no display suggesting a police shoot-out on a farmhouse's front porch.

Like anybody who'd lived in the area for any time at all didn't automatically connect this farm with murder.

And like the edginess of something-really-bad-happened-here wasn't the real reason Cristanis Farm's haunted hayride did better than any other in the area.

The reason the Spagnola sisters were harassing Ashley was because this barn, built by Nikko's grandfather when he had still had high hopes for the land, was constructed on the one section of the farm that wasn't given over to the new house or its front lawn, or apple orchard, or crop fields—the spot that had been cleared already because that was where the original Roehmar house had stood.

"I'm doing fine," Ashley assured one and all through the headset.

And she was, too.

Until the light went out.

There must have been a lightning strike that hit something important causing all the lights in the area to go out: After one moment of startled silence, Ashley could hear the chatter as everyone connected by the headsets whooped, as though this was just another special effect thought up by Nikko.

Another flash of lightning, and Ashley blinked because of the brightness of the lightning—and in the darkness afterward saw someone framed in the doorway of the barn.

"Ramon?" she called.

No answer.

Could Karl or any of the others be touchy enough to remain silent because she'd guessed wrong?

She reached down to the far side of the hay bale she was lying on and scrabbled for the flashlight the Cristanises provided for walking from one site on the farm to the other. Just as her fingers closed on the flashlight, she felt the tug of the wire that attached the earpiece to battery pack. And then she didn't feel it and knew that she'd pulled the wire loose, but that was not her immediate concern.

She pressed the flashlight's switch and swung the light toward the doorway.

Where no one was standing.

She could make out the bales of hay, the farm implements since—besides the haunted hayrides—this was a real working barn, the posed dummies, the hanged man spinning slowly in the breeze. But there was no one in the doorway.

As there shouldn't be.

Maybe it was some weird afterimage left by the

lightning and induced by the Halloween atmosphere on the farm or by thinking of the guys Morgan Roehmar had murdered. Or she'd seen the hanged man and, trick of the shifting light, he'd seemed farther away, in the doorway.

Or maybe whoever it was had stepped away into the darkness outside.

Still sitting on the bale of hay, Ashley flicked the flashlight so the beam of light hit the battery pack, the wire that should have been stretched out to the earpiece lying limp on the floor.

Aiming the light back at the doorway, she set the flashlight next to her and picked up both pieces of the headset. Glancing up repeatedly to make sure whoever it was—if there *was* a whoever—couldn't sneak up on her, she tried to thread the jagged end of wire back into what she thought was the appropriate hole of the earpiece, but there wasn't even static.

Okay, so there was no calling for help.

If help was needed.

Ashley sincerely hoped her paranoia was in overdrive.

Still, it was no good to try to simply *hope* danger away. If someone was lurking out there, ignoring him was not going to make him go away. She picked up the flashlight and moved to the doorway of the barn. The rain was still beating down, giving the air a fresh, clean smell, but making a muddy puddle of the entryway.

No footprints in the mud.

Was the force of the rain enough to wash away footprints in the time—surely no more than thirty seconds—she had delayed, to check the headset?

She shone the flashlight into the darkness outside, but most of the light bounced off the sheets of rain, not making it to the trees several hundred feet away.

A well-timed bolt of lightning lit up the entire area just as a simultaneous crack of thunder jarred her teeth—and there wasn't a trace of anyone.

Of course, whoever it was—again, *if* there'd been a whoever—could have circled around to the back of the barn.

But there wasn't anyone, Ashley told herself. The tractor drivers kept a count of how many people were in each wagon, because Nikko would have frowned on their losing a customer. Who would be wandering around the farm on such a miserable night? The workers had all sought shelter; the customers were presumably accounted for.

Still, she pulled the barn doors shut, which was only a sensible precaution in case the wind shifted, but she was very aware that the latch and padlock were on the outside because there was never any reason to lock yourself into a barn, only to close it up after yourself. On this side there was just a piece of twine fastened to one door, whose loop end slipped over a block of wood nailed into the other door—protection against the wind swinging the doors wide open, but hardly security against someone wanting to get in.

Facing the doors as she fastened the twine, Ashley felt a tingle in the spot between her shoulder blades. A somebody's-behind-you-watching-you sort of feeling. And she realized that the person she'd half convinced herself she hadn't seen in the doorway could have ducked down when she blinked.

And could have gotten back up again while she stood looking in the totally wrong direction.

She whipped around, the beam of her flashlight skittering over Anne Boleyn's head, the hanged man, the man tied to the chair, the knife-wielding man she thought of as *her* murderer.

Nothing.

She played the light up in the loft. Nikko hadn't put anything up there this year, because last year's mannequin hadn't worked well—a man sitting on the edge, holding a gun to his head. When that year's barn attendant would turn the light on, there was a tape recording of a gunshot, then the man fell backward so that only his feet, still dangling over the edge, showed. Or at least that was the theory. Several times he didn't fall far enough, which looked lame. Once he fell forward and off, almost hitting the people in the wagon, not only exposing the mannequin's wires but—Nikko's father supposedly ranted—also exposing Cristanis Family Farm to a potential lawsuit. So now there were only a couple bats and world-class–sized spiders dangling from the edge of the loft.

Were they vibrating more than they should have from the wind and from her closing the doors?

No way, Ashley told herself, could someone have climbed up that ladder in the short time she'd had her back turned.

And she would have heard.

Wouldn't she?

The rain was still hitting the back of the barn with enough force that it almost sounded like hail.

She walked around the downstairs section, circling the mannequins, the bales of hay, shining her flashlight into each gloomy corner.

There was definitely no one down here.

The doors rattled.

But that was just the wind.

She was fairly sure.

She shone the light up into the loft again and weighed her options. It was almost impossible that anybody was up there, but she knew she couldn't remain in this barn without making sure. There was probably nobody outside, either, but that was more plausible than that there was somebody in here. If she left the barn, to get away from the person who probably wasn't in the loft, she might run into the person who might be outside. And, more likely, she could have a lightning-struck branch fall on her, or she could trip and twist her ankle from the slickness underfoot, or she could catch pneumonia. And she'd have to explain why she'd left the barn, and the others would know how badly spooked she'd been, and they'd laugh at her and say she was too young to work here after all.

There is, she assured herself, *nobody in the loft.*

She looked around for a weapon. Just in case. The pitchfork in chair-guy's chest, the ax that had severed Anne Boleyn's head, the knife held by the man murdering the wench—all those were plastic. There had to be a real pitchfork somewhere around the barn, but it was put away so nobody could hurt themselves with it.

As she was likely to do—even if she could find it—if she tried climbing the ladder with it.

Ashley wound the wire from the headset's battery

pack around her hand, figuring she could climb with that and, potentially, use it to smack any intruder. She put her foot on the lowest rung of the ladder and realized the flashlight made climbing dangerous. It was too fat: She couldn't hold it *and* get a secure grip on the ladder. What good would she accomplish if she proved to herself she was alone but fell to her death doing so? She tried holding the end of the flashlight in her mouth, but—besides being gross—she was too likely to gag.

So she set the flashlight down on the floor, pointing up into the loft so she could see.

Ashley once more set foot onto the lowest rung. She took a steadying breath, then climbed all in a rush, hesitating only when the top of her head came even with the floor of the loft.

She gave a quick peek.

Nothing *waiting* for her, anyway.

She scrambled the rest of the way up, then swung the battery pack, just in case anyone came lunging out of one of the corners. But the only thing it made contact with was her own wrist.

See, she chided herself.

Then she *did* see it, a crouched figure in the right-hand corner. The light from the flashlight was too dim for her to make out any details. She swung the battery pack again, and it broke loose from the wire, hitting the floor down below with a dull thud. But the shadow didn't approach, or move. Or make a sound.

That gave her the courage to take a step closer.

It was the stupid suicidal dummy from last year, abandoned and shoved into this far corner in disgrace.

Ashley realized how raggedly she had been breathing.

It smelled of dusty heat up here, despite the coolness of the October night, the air thick and hard to breathe.

But she stayed long enough to check behind the dummy, behind the hay bales—though nothing bigger than a medium-sized dog could have hidden behind them. Still. Just to be sure.

She was embarrassed with herself for being as silly as a grade-school kid scaring herself with her own campfire story. The storm was still close, but moving away, though it had brought a cold front in with it. But the force of the rain was lessening, and most people would rather see the show even if it was cold and drizzling out. If Nikko was right about no other light-ning in the area . . .

But, no, she realized as she climbed back down the ladder: The show couldn't resume until the electricity came back on. Whether it did or the show was canceled, somebody should be noticing soon that they weren't getting any responses from her over their headsets.

Nikko would send someone to check on her, and she would have to admit to breaking the headset. Maybe she could come up with a good explanation before then, an explanation that wouldn't make her sound like a klutz or like a baby, spooked by shadows.

She was unwrapping the battery pack wire from around her fingers as she turned to face the door, to pick up the flashlight. Beyond the circle of light aimed past her at the loft, she saw a figure standing in the barn, in front of one of the doors, the doors that were still fastened by twine.

Not the hanged man. Definitely not another left-over dummy.

But even as she backed away she noticed things. Like that he was not a man, but a boy about her age, or at the most a year or two older. Which, of course, did not make him any less dangerous. Despite the light from the flashlight shining in her eyes, she could see him clearly enough to make out that his hair was dry, not dripping in his face as it would have to be in this downpour.

Then lightning flashed, not that close, but visible through the gap between the barn doors, enough to illuminate where the boy stood.

Except there was no boy.

Then the barn was dark again.

And he was back.

He flung his arm up to protect his eyes, then whispered, "Please don't hurt me."

It was a relief, of sorts, that he was afraid of her, except that she knew animals sometimes attacked out of fear. Still, it indicated he hadn't come in here planning on hurting her. Except how could he have gotten in? How could he disappear in lightning that wasn't bright enough to dazzle her eyes?

Ashley darted forward, grabbed the flashlight, and swung the beam in his direction.

He disappeared. Like a movie that fades off the projection screen when the overhead lights come on, he paled into nothingness.

There was no reasonable explanation for that.

Ashley backed up and tripped over one of the bales of hay, so that she sat down, hard and fast, her bottom skimming the edge of the bale, which scraped her back on her way down to the floor. The beam of light jerked up and down—over the doors, onto the floor—but she knew to hold tight, and she didn't drop the flashlight.

In the half moments the light was not shining on him, the boy reappeared, crouching on the floor, his arms over his head as though warding off a blow.

Ashley tasted blood and realized she'd bitten her lip. She watched the shadow cast by the hanged man, creeping over the far wall, over the door, as he twisted in the air currents, silent except for the creaking of the beam. She was amazed she could hear that little sound over the pounding of her heart.

"Who are you?" Ashley demanded of the boy who was no longer there. "What do you want?"

Thunder grumbled, off in the distance, but the boy didn't answer.

Ashley felt she knew who he had to be, though her rational mind kept trying to push that possibility away.

He was a dead boy, one of Morgan Roehmar's victims. Brought back . . . by what? The electricity of the storm? The particular night? Some alignment of the planets?

By the lack of light, definitely. Ashley kept a firm hold of the flashlight.

Then thought about all the dark corners of the barn behind her.

Still sitting on the floor, she swung the flashlight in an arc around her.

And once more glimpsed the boy by the doors as her beam of light chased the darkness around the barn.

He was gone once she aimed the flashlight directly in front of her again.

So, apparently something confined him to that spot. Good.

She sat with the comforting realness of the bale of hay pressing against her back and tried to keep her teeth from chattering.

C'mon, Nikko, she thought.

Ramon.

Somebody.

Morgan Roehmar had lured boys into trusting him—good-looking boys, the talk went, though of course the original news coverage had been way before her time. And she had never paid attention when, every so often, there would be a retrospective in the newspapers, usually on the anniversary of the day Roehmar held police at bay for almost twelve hours before a police sharpshooter had picked him off from where he'd barricaded himself on his front porch. Even as the coroner carried his dead body out, the dogs the police had brought into the house had gone frantic, finding the two bodies the girlfriend had told the police might be there, but still the dogs wouldn't settle down till they found another. Then another. Then another. Five bodies all told, or six—Ashley couldn't even remember. It was a story for campfires, for Halloween, for parents to warn their kids with, saying, "Even here, in a quiet place like this . . ."

The boy Ashley had glimpsed had been good-looking, what she'd seen of him before he'd dropped into a defensive crouch.

She tried to remember the details. She remembered the high school runner, because there was a picture of him still up in the trophy case outside the gym all these years later. This hadn't been him. The migrant worker? He hadn't seemed dark enough, but maybe. She thought there'd been a younger boy, twelve or thirteen, tricked by Roehmar asking for help finding a lost puppy—but that might be confusing two stories into one. And she was drawing a total blank on the other two, or possibly three, guys.

The only face she could truly remember from the papers was Roehmar's—he'd been in his fifties, kind of jowly but clean-shaven. Not much hair on top of his head, either, and what was there was gray. Ashley had always thought there was an intrinsically evil look about his eyes, but maybe that came from afterward, from knowing what he did, for he didn't seem to have trouble fooling people. Somehow or other—and he had different ways for the different boys over the several years and several counties he'd done this— Roehmar tricked his victims into trusting him long enough to overpower them, then he tied them up and strangled them with electrical wire.

No wonder this kid was acting terrified. The last few minutes of his life must have been awful.

Which was no reason for him to hang around frightening her.

But she couldn't get his words out of her head: "Please don't hurt me."

There'd been nobody to help him then. Could she help him now?

There's nothing you can do, she told herself.

Nothing to save his life, obviously. But why was his spirit—his ghost, whatever (she felt silly even thinking the words to herself)—still here? Something must be wrong.

Well, duh.

Something *beyond* that he'd been killed in a terrible way. *All* the boys had been killed in a terrible way. Why was this one still here—she again cringed at the wording—haunting?

No matter where Roehmar killed them—and the police suspected it hadn't been at the house—afterward he brought the bodies back to the farm, cut them into manageable pieces, wrapped them in plastic bags, and shoved them into the basement's crawl space. Even when the police had come in response to the girlfriend's complaint, they had originally just been going through the motions required to follow up on her accusation—not taking her seriously until Roehmar freaked out.

But he *had* freaked out. And so he had been killed. The bodies had been brought out of their hiding place, identified, buried. Though their murderer had never been brought to trial, he *had* been brought to justice.

Ashley flicked the beam of light away from the door, revealing the kid once more. He had sat down on the floor, his arms encircling his knees, which were drawn up to his chest. He was rocking back and forth, watching her. Unable to stand it, Ashley aimed the flashlight directly at him again.

She could get a priest, she thought, to come out here and bless the place.

Yeah, right. And she would get the priest out here by telling him what, exactly? *Bless me, Father, for I have seen a ghost . . .*

She turned the flashlight away from him once more. "What do you want?" she demanded, recognizing that her voice came out harshly.

He *was* good-looking: dark hair, huge dark eyes. He swallowed hard before answering, in a little voice, "I want to go home."

The flashlight shook in Ashley's hand, making the

hanged man's shadow dance, but she kept the beam of light away from the area by the doors.

Does he know he's dead? she wondered. She didn't dare ask, for fear that such knowledge might make a ghost more powerful, more malevolent. Or was the lack of knowledge precisely what was keeping him here? Ashley just didn't know how all this supernatural stuff worked. So she only repeated, "'Home'?"

"Don't let him hurt me anymore," the kid said.

"He won't," Ashley assured him. "He can't."

At least the kid stopped rocking. "Why didn't they take me?" he asked. "Why did they take the others but not me?"

That was a chill up her back. "Who are you?"

The boy began rocking again. Though he looked Ashley's age, his fear made him appear much younger. "I can't remember," he cried in desperation. "Everything's fading away from me." He held his hands out to her. "Like with the light."

She could see through him: She could see his torso through his hands, the door through his torso. She angled the flashlight's beam farther away from him, and the lack of light made him easier to see.

"At least there were the others before," he said, and Ashley wondered if Roehmar had kept one boy alive longer than the rest, though she had never heard anything like that, but then he added, "the ones in the crawl space. But they took them away, and they left me."

"Where are you?" Ashley asked. Dumb question, he was obviously right in front of her in the barn.

But he didn't say that. He said: "Here. Under the porch."

Her breath came in a hiss.

There was another body.

The police had found the plastic bags under the floorboards, crammed into the crawl space. And they'd already found more than they had thought to find. But there was another. Buried in the ground. The house had stood empty, then been knocked down; the barn had eventually gone up in the same place—but without a foundation, without digging.

"Can't they come again to get me?" he pleaded. "Can't you show them?"

"Yes," she assured him.

"Will you stay with me until . . ."—she suspected he altered the direction of his question—"until then?"

"Of course." Though it was the last thing in the world she wanted to do.

Nikko, or whoever he sent to check up on her, would come bearing flashlights, but she would make them turn the lights off, and then they would see. She would not be silly, easily spooked Ashley, but Ashley who had solved a mystery, who was helping to lay a spirit to rest.

"Can you call them to come now?" the lost boy asked.

"My headset's broken," she explained.

"I'm good . . . I used to be good . . ."—the kid closed his eyes—"with electronic stuff."

She went back to gather the parts: earpiece, loose wire, and battery pack. The thunder was a distant grumble now; she could hear the water dripping off the roof, but no longer the sound of rain battering the barn or the ground. Help would be here soon enough, but she couldn't bear to tell the poor dead kid to wait any longer than he already had. "Can you touch . . ." *Um, how did one word THAT?* "Solid things?"

"Sometimes," the boy replied from his seat by the door, so weak and wistful she worried he was about to fade away again. If he did, how would she ever know when he'd come back so she could rescue him?

She rushed back to the door and crouched beside him. He looked more solid than ever, and when she leaned in close, her hand brushed his arm, and she felt it—she *felt* it, though before she'd seen the light pass through him. "How's this?" she asked, holding the earpiece in one hand and the battery pack and the loose wire in the other. The flashlight was back where she'd left it, turned away from the door, beyond the hanged man.

"Fine," he said. His hand touched hers—*touched hers*—as he picked up the wire and stretched it out. "Fine," he repeated. Then, moving quicker than she'd have thought possible, he wrapped the wire around her neck and began to squeeze.

Ashley clawed at his face, but that just made him tighten the wire even more brutally.

"Stupid girl," he hissed into her ear. "I hate stupid, treacherous girls."

He jerked the wire with each word until the room was spinning. She clawed at her own neck, trying to get her fingers beneath the wire, away from her throat, but it was cutting into her, cutting off her breath, cutting off her ability to think—except for the one thought over and over, *How can this be? How can this be?*—until there were no thoughts anymore, no breath, no . . .

Morgan Roehmar let the girl's dead body slump against his and felt the excitement that killing always brought. She *was* stupid. Why in the world did she assume a ghost would choose to look the way its body had looked at the moment of death—all bloody or diseased?

Or old? He much preferred to take on the form of the way he had looked at seventeen—the age of the boys he'd killed. But that had been a mistake, killing boys, he now knew, thinking of the woman who had betrayed him to the police, thinking of this one.

He was stronger, now that he'd killed her, and he'd get stronger with each additional death. Already he was no longer limited to the area where the porch had been, where he'd died. Though he had no access to a chain saw, or to plastic bags, he did have time, before people would come with their damn lights that would scatter him in the air. He laid her out on that bale of hay beneath the mannequin with the knife, with her peasant dress arranged artfully about her, her hands folded just below her bosom, the earpiece over her head, the battery-pack wire entwined around her fingers the way a funeral home placed rosary beads.

Nice and neat.

Ready for her friends to find her.

For there was nothing, Morgan Roehmar thought, worse than a messy dead body.

ONLY ON
ALL HALLOWS' EVE

As far as Martin could tell, the village of Farnham was too small to have anything interesting ever happen. Sixteen years of living in Farnham was enough to make anyone's brain begin to slumber, but Martin was determined not to let this happen to him, as it had so obviously happened to all the elders of the village, and to so many of his kinsfolk, and was now beginning to happen to his age-mates.

Even his cousin Raleigh, who had always been good for thinking up schemes and pranks and ways to get out of working any more than was absolutely necessary, even Raleigh was no longer fun. Lately he was taken with Lissa, the blacksmith's daughter, and all of a sudden he was concerned about not looking foolish, or lazy, and he was absorbed with searching out opportunities to talk with her, and—failing that—to talking *about* her.

It was enough to make Martin a bit desperate.

The last almost-exciting thing to happen in Farnham was during the summer when old man Tomlin had run away from home to join the army—or, depending on who was telling the story, to get away from his old scold of a wife, Elfirda.

Yet when Martin expressed the thought that maybe army life would be more appealing than farming, Raleigh—who seemed intent on turning into someone's grandmother—countered that no one ever thought to see old Tomlin alive again. Soldiering, he said, was sure to get a body killed much faster than boredom ever did.

Then, in the fall, as the season of harvesting was drawing to a close, and a long, hard winter of cold days and dark nights was all there was to look forward to, a holy man named Brother Wade came to the village.

Farnham was too small to have a church or a priest, but occasionally preachers would visit and use Martin's father's tavern as a gathering place to give their sermons. The fact that Brother Wade was someone new was the exciting thing—not his sermon, for Brother Wade talked about Purgatory, where the souls that were not quite ready for Heaven waited. This was not a subject that Martin craved to learn more about.

"It is our job," Brother Wade said, "the job of us, the Church on Earth, to join with the saints who have gone before us and pray for those souls in Purgatory.

Purgatory is an in-between place—not Heaven, not Hell, not of Earth, but buried deep in the center of the earth."

Finally, Brother Wade said something interesting: "Come All Hallows' Eve, the gates of Purgatory open, and the souls fly out and enter Heaven, where they join the saints and become the Church Triumphant. If you're watchful on All Hallows' Eve, you may catch a glimpse of your loved ones who have died that year as they make their way from Purgatory, through Earth, and up to Heaven."

Martin hadn't ever heard this before.

Martin's father didn't care for Brother Wade. It was his father's custom to provide free ale to the holy men who passed through Farnham. But none had stayed as long or drank as much as Brother Wade. "And," Martin's father complained to the family, "I never heard anyone explain Purgatory in quite that way before. I'm not even sure he has it right."

Martin, too, found it hard to picture Brother Wade's description of the dead souls coming up through the ground on All Hallows' Eve and walking among the living one final time before breaking the bonds of Earth and floating up to Heaven. Martin had lived through sixteen All Hallows' Eves, and he had never yet seen a spirit walk, that night or any other.

Still, Brother Wade's discourse suggested a plan to Martin, a plan that was so good it was sure to shake Raleigh out of his Lissa-induced lethargy.

"I have a wonderful idea," Martin told Raleigh that afternoon, "for a trick to play on mean old Elfirda tonight." In truth, Elfirda was no older than his parents, but she was as sullen and cranky as a toothache. She always chased the village boys away from her property, not letting them take the shortcut to the stream, where they liked to swim on hot summer days. And every autumn, she accused them of stealing apples from her trees, when everyone could see there were too many for her and her equally ill-tempered husband to ever eat on their own. And now that Tomlin was gone, Elfirda was practically drowning in apples and should have been happy to rid herself of some. But she was as stingy with them as ever. Now, on this day of Brother Wade's sermon, Martin had seen how distraught Elfirda looked when Brother Wade talked about catching a glimpse of recently dead loved ones, for—like everyone else—she must assume Tomlin had probably gotten himself killed by now. This looked like a fine opportunity to get back at her.

"Aw, leave the old biddy alone," Raleigh said. "It has to have been hard for her this past year, with her husband abandoning her and leaving her on her own. She has enough misery without us to add to it."

"Well, of course, Tomlin left the old nag," Martin said. "The wonder is that he stayed as long as he did."

Raleigh was still shaking his head.

Martin said, "You can be the ghost of old man Tomlin. I'll run up ahead of you to Elfirda's cottage and tell her I've seen you, that you must have died in the war, and you're on your way from Purgatory to Heaven. That way I'll put the idea in her head that you're Tomlin, and we won't have to worry overmuch that you're taller and not so broad as he was." This was a great concession on Martin's part since *Martin*, in fact, *was* the right size.

"Naw," Raleigh said. "It's a low trick. Besides, I promised Lissa—"

"But this is All Hallows' Eve. Your plans for her can wait another night. Tonight is our one and only chance for this."

"Still . . . ," Raleigh said, shaking his head.

"Never mind, then." Martin stalked away, disgusted that—once again—Lissa was all Raleigh could think about.

But it was such a good plan, Martin couldn't resist, even without his cousin.

When he got home, and while his mother's back was turned, Martin fetched some flour from the drum where his mother kept it. That night, after the rest of his family had gone to bed, he rubbed it onto his face and hands to make himself look pale and gray. Next, he smashed some berries onto a rag, which he wrapped around his head so that it looked like a bloody bandage—with the added benefit that it also covered his dark hair and a good deal of his face. It would not convince Elfirda should she get a good look at him, but his intention was to only let her catch a glimpse.

Silently he crawled out the window of his parents' house and into All Hallows' Eve night. He delayed only to go to a place where the stream gathered in an elbow of land, where the water was stagnant. He rinsed his shirt in that water, giving it the stench of death, which would help convince Elfirda that he was her departed husband.

Then, as the moon hung low in the sky, Martin went to old lady Elfirda's cottage. He scratched at her window shutter, whispering in a hoarse voice, "Elfie, Elfie," which is what Tomlin had always called her. *That* should startle her awake and out of bed, but still give him time to run away. "Elfie, Elfie, come and bid your husband good-bye."

All in all, it was a very good disguise.

What Martin had no way of knowing was that Elfirda wasn't in bed, or even in the cottage, but instead had been tending her cow in the barn, for it had injured its foot.

Nor did he see her come up behind him and bend to pick a rock up off the ground.

The last thing he heard was her crackly voice muttering, "Drat, I killed you once and pushed your body in the stream to rid myself of you. Why would I want to say good-bye again?"

CEMETERY FIELD TRIP

Janelle hardly listened as Ms. Hurston gave the same lecture all teachers all over the world always give every time there's a field trip:

- Don't be an embarrassment to the school.
- Don't litter.
- Don't damage anything.
- Don't damage each other.
- Don't get lost.

Janelle and the other nineteen students in Ms. Hurston's fifth-period ninth-grade literature class yawned all the way through this.

Then, because they *were* ninth graders, Ms. Hurston added:

- No smoking.
- No drinking.
- No wandering off as couples.

Because they were ninth graders, the kids tittered.

Then, because they were going to a cemetery, Ms. Hurston repeated the rule about not being an embarrassment.

"Remember," she said, standing in the front of the bus, swaying every time they went around a corner or over a bump, "even though we're going to be in the part of the cemetery where there are mostly old graves, there *are* recent interments, too, and there might be people there visiting their loved ones."

Brandon, who—as far as Janelle was concerned—had been a pain in the butt since she'd first met him in third grade, said, "Yeah, and besides, it's Halloween." He wiggled his eyebrows and—just in case anybody didn't get it—explained, "And on Halloween there's no way to know if someone you meet in a cemetery is *visiting* or *staying*." Again the eyebrows wiggled.

Brandon's warning got some of the girls giddy, and some of the boys trying to outdo one another in graphic details about what those who stayed in a cemetery might look like.

Grow up, Janelle wished at them. She thought this whole trip was creepy enough as it was.

If Ms. Hurston was thinking the same thing, she didn't say so. She said, as though correcting an honest misconception, "Actually, Brandon— Jake, if you fall

CEMETERY FIELD TRIP

out the window, we're not stopping the bus to pick you up. Actually, we are not on the lookout for ghosts, ghouls, or hordes of the undead lurking in wait to suck our brains out through our eye sockets." While some of the kids made disappointed noises, Ms. Hurston went on, "Speaking of eye sockets, D'Vona, can you put the mascara away until the bus stops, so that you don't poke your eye out? Anybody remember why we're going to Mount Hope Cemetery today?"

Janelle joined the others in not meeting Ms. Hurston's gaze. Of course, they *knew*: She'd told them three times this morning alone. But nobody wanted to act like they *cared*.

Ms. Hurston asked, "Are we here just to avoid sixth-period algebra?"

"Reason enough," someone from the back of the bus called.

"I want you to look for specific details," Ms. Hurston reminded them. "This cemetery was started in the 1800s. That was the Victorian era. Remember the Victorian poetry we've been studying all month? Anyone? Tennyson, Rossetti, the two Brownings?" She shook her head at the lack of response and joked, "Never heard of any of them before."

Because she was generally a pretty cool teacher, they were willing to take it as a joke.

Ms. Hurston reminded them, "Victorians believed cemeteries should be parklike to encourage people to come, to consider their mortality. And they were very big into symbolism."

The Victorians, Janelle thought, *with the possible exception of Christina Rossetti, were downright weird.*

The bus passed through the stone gateway, then parked by the fountain.

"Notice details," Ms. Hurston said as they gathered up their hats and gloves, for the day was overcast and chilly.

The students noticed the fountain with its lion-head spigots, though nobody was able to determine to everyone's satisfaction exactly what they were supposed to symbolize.

They discussed, under Ms. Hurston's guidance, the plants around the fountain: what was still blooming at what, for upstate New York, was the very end of the growing season, and which were flowers that wouldn't come again till spring.

They speculated about—after he left—the creepy-looking guy in the shapeless hat and the long tweed coat, who hadn't come close but who had glowered at them when they weren't even doing anything: just standing there listening to Ms. Hurston and looking at . . . well, some of them were climbing onto . . . the fountain. "A homeless person," they decided, because of the long, stringy gray hair, and because of the shapeless clothes that gave the impression of being layered over another whole set of clothes. Either that or a crazed mass murderer stalking them.

Ms. Hurston told them they were so politically incorrect they made her eyes cross, which she demonstrated for them.

"Okay, now we're heading into the old section." Ms. Hurston pointed toward a brick road that wound its way up a hill. "Susan B. Anthony's grave is in this section, and Nathaniel Rochester, who founded Rochester. Let's see if we can find them. But keep your eyes, ears, and noses open for sensory details. There won't be an assignment, but there will be a discussion. Notice things!"

"Yeah, well," Janelle muttered to Reid, "what I notice is that bricks are very hard to walk on." Even with sneakers, her ankles wobbled on the uneven surface, and she worried that if she rushed, she might trip and make a fool of herself. So already she was bringing up the rear, except for Reid, who had stopped to tie his shoelace.

The oldest gravestones were thin slabs of limestone—bright white where they weren't spotted by gray-green lichen growing on them—and so eroded by weather or by people making rubbings that they were almost illegible. The granite and marble stones were generally in better shape, and it was easier to see some of those symbols Ms. Hurston was so eager to have them notice.

"Wow," Brandon said, "all these people really got stoned."

Ms. Hurston ignored him. "See these ferns?" she asked, and Janelle ran her finger in the engraving. Each type of headstone—marble, granite, limestone—felt totally different from one another. Janelle noted this for possible sharing in case she got called on to say something.

"Ferns symbolize sorrow," Ms. Hurston said. "As does the willow. And this calla lily—that symbolizes marriage."

"What about these three interlocking rings?" D'Vona asked.

Brandon said, "That's for someone who made it only partway through the Olympics."

"Holy Trinity," Ms. Hurston corrected. "What about this flower bud?"

They shook their heads.

"Same as a lamb," she prompted.

"A kid?" someone asked.

It was hard to keep on laughing and joking at the thought of a dead kid.

Ms. Hurston nodded. "A child under the age of twelve. So a partially opened bloom?"

"Is for a teenager."

That was an even ickier feeling: someone their own age.

There were several graves with the same last name. Judging by the dates, it looked as though the parents in that family had outlived all their children.

"What do you think these crossed swords mean?" Ms. Hurston asked.

"Soldier?" somebody asked.

"More than that. Notice the date he died."

1863.

Was the Civil War still going on then? Janelle suspected she wasn't the only one who couldn't be sure. Still, somebody took the plunge and guessed, "Killed in battle."

Ms. Hurston nodded.

Janelle noticed the partial bloom, and that made her look at the other date—the "born in" date. "He was fifteen," she pointed out.

Hard as it was to think of someone their age being dead, it was even harder to think of someone their age dying in battle.

Jake asked, "What about those big . . ."

Ms. Hurston supplied the word: "Mausoleums."

"Can we go in?"

"They'll be locked, but we can look in the window."

"Eww," Xavier said.

Courtney, who had a crush on Xavier, echoed, *"Eww."*

But everybody else crowded around to see.

The mausoleum was about the size of a backyard storage shed, but it looked like a tiny little chapel. A tiny little *deserted* chapel. There was a set of doors, which were padlocked shut, and each had a window of smoke-colored leaded glass. The windows were dirty and cobwebby, and one had a hole that looked as though it had been shot with a BB gun.

Somehow or other, Janelle and D'Vona ended up being first in line to peek in. Standing behind, Brandon asked, in his best attempt at a spooky voice, "Is that lock to keep us out, or to keep them in?"

"Shut up," Janelle said. She stood on her tiptoes but didn't want to put her face near the dirty glass. "Too dark to see anything," she said, giving her place up to Reid.

But D'Vona, who hadn't moved, said, "Cool!"

"What do you see?" those in the back asked. "Are there bodies?"

"Coffins," Reid said. "On these, like, shelves."

When Jake took D'Vona's place, he said what Janelle had thought: "I don't see anything."

"You gotta give your eyes a chance to adjust," D'Vona and Reid said. D'Vona demonstrated by holding her hands up to the sides of her face. "Block the light from outside, and then all of a sudden it's like the shapes just form in the darkness."

Janelle had to wait until everybody else was through to get a second chance. This time she didn't rush. In a few seconds, the details came out of the gloom: six dark boxes, three on each side, stacked like in a supermarket—the coffin aisle. "Now I see," she said.

Nobody commented, and when she stepped back, she saw that everyone else had moved on.

She could still see them—they hadn't wandered off that far, but they'd divided.

Despite the fact that they had, indeed, seen some graves that were only two or three or five years old in this section, she and her classmates were the only visitors in this part of the cemetery. The day was probably too cold for anyone who hadn't ordered a bus three weeks in advance, and the trees were pretty much bare—so not very photogenic.

Janelle shuffled her feet through the leaves. *Notice the details,* she reminded herself. Ms. Hurston had this thing about class participation. The leaves were no longer crisp and colorful, and they had hardly any of that wonderful autumn smell to them. Concentrating on details, Janelle tripped over a marker, so low it had been hidden by the leaves, and she fell to her knees.

"You okay?" Brandon—of all people—called over to her.

"Just tying my shoelace," Janelle said. When she was sure no one was looking, she rubbed her sore knee.

Her classmates continued on, distracted by different things.

"Look," Xavier called. "I wonder how old this is." He was heading toward a grave that had a little flag stuck into the ground.

At the same time, Alycia, from across one of the little cemetery roads, said, "Here's a whole bunch of Rochesters, but I don't see Nathaniel."

And Ms. Hurston was all excited because there were three graves with quotes from Emerson on them. She and the kids who were either the poetry-loving kind or suck-ups were reading them out loud.

Janelle tried to find something interesting that she could call people's attention to.

She leaned in to read a gravestone, but there was nothing special about it: a man's name, the year of his birth—1877—and the year of his death, 1920. No other inscription, no decoration.

What kind of decoration would I want on my headstone? she thought. It was hard to come up with something for herself. For Reid, a football, since he was a defensive lineman on the school team. A Gameboy for D'Vona. For Brandon . . . A simple etching would never be enough for Brandon; they would have to figure out some way to attach to the stone one of those gag flowers that squirt water.

She was smiling at that thought when she heard a sound.

Was that a cat? she wondered.

They had seen, in the distance, back when they first went up the bricked road, a young couple jogging with their black Labrador retriever, but at the moment, she couldn't see anybody besides her classmates.

And, of course, people didn't generally take their cats jogging.

She looked around to find where the sound was coming from and heard it again—a weak, pathetic mew.

Janelle revised her first impression—a kitten, she thought now. She wondered how far the cemetery extended in this direction. Could there be houses backing up to it? Could a kitten have wandered out of somebody's yard and gotten lost here?

Or had some heartless soul abandoned an unwanted pet?

Her mind flashed a picture of the jogging couple. She tried not to think of their dog—or anybody's dog—finding the kitten.

Janelle walked in a circle, keeping her gaze on where blown leaves had accumulated into little piles near gravestones. A poor, lost kitten might have settled into such a place to get out of the wind.

The sound came again, and this time, because she was listening for it, Janelle determined it came from behind her.

"Here, kitty, kitty," she called softly, so as not to frighten the poor creature.

Past the grave of the man who had died in 1920, past the place where she had tripped.

"Here, kitty, kitty."

She glanced back over her shoulder and could see only a few of her classmates; the others had already gone down the hill where the road curved, which was the direction those she could still see were heading now, too.

She was just about to say to herself, *Well, too bad, kitten,* when she heard it again. Much closer this time.

It seemed to be coming from behind the mausoleum they had all peeked into.

Oh, kitten, she thought, with another glance toward her classmates.

They couldn't get that far away from her, she thought. And even if, once she had rescued the kitten and then reached the hill, *even if* they had gone off so far that she couldn't tell which direction they had gone, she could always go back and wait for them on the bus.

Which would at least be nice and warm and out of the wind.

Janelle walked up to the mausoleum. The name BALSEN was engraved over the doorway. Janelle purposefully didn't look into the windows. She didn't want to experience again their disconcerting way of hiding, then revealing, the shelves inside. And what the shelves held.

Instead she walked around to the back. There, the names of six Balsens were listed: Frederick Jeremiah Balsen, Carolyn Balsen Vandenhoof, Faustine Balsen, Winslowe Childs Balsen, Robert Marwin Balsen, Margaret St. Claire Balsen-Timmons, along with their dates. The most recent Balsen was Margaret, who had died in 1943, but Janelle didn't take the time to try to figure out their relationships.

There was no sign of a kitten.

But the pathetic little mew came again.

Janelle closed her eyes. "Oh great," she muttered. The sound was definitely coming from directly on the other side of the mausoleum wall—from inside.

Now would be the time to give up on that kitten.

Except, *now,* this close, she could no longer be certain it *was* a kitten.

In fact, she was certain it was not.

It was a baby, a newborn baby.

She was sure because her cousin and his wife had just had a baby, and this was exactly what their infant sounded like. And while a kitten *might* have found a tiny opening to squeeze in through, there was no way a baby could have gotten inside by itself. There was also no way Janelle could decide, *Well, I don't really need to do anything—it's sure to find its way back.* Someone, probably a frightened, unwed teenager, had had a baby, and had abandoned it here.

But the door was padlocked shut.

We would have seen a baby, she told herself.

Yet she remembered it had been only by *knowing* there was something—it had only been by staring into the gloom—that she had been able to make out the coffins.

Janelle knew she absolutely needed to get Ms. Hurston back here.

But when she stepped out from behind the mausoleum, her classmates were all out of sight. To get help, she would have to run across this section of the cemetery and down the hill. She would have to try to find the others—when it may or may not have been obvious which direction they had gone.

What if, after all that, she couldn't find them? Then she'd have to go back to the bus and tell the driver.

And all the while, she'd have to hope she would be able to find this particular mausoleum again.

Of course I could find it again, she told herself.

And then—also *of course*—everyone would laugh at her because there'd be no way to get into the locked mausoleum. But they wouldn't need to get in to find out that she was wrong about the baby, or the kitten—that it wasn't either of those things. It was only . . .

Who knew? Something else.

But, still. The thought of a baby, a poor, unwanted baby, who had been here who-could-guess-how-long already, lying in the cold and dark among those dead bodies . . .

The thought of those dead bodies made Janelle pause.

Brandon's words came back to her—*Thank you very much, Brandon*—about it being Halloween and about Halloween being a day when you couldn't be sure about the people you met in a cemetery.

She looked again at the names and dates on the back wall. *Don't let one of them be a newborn baby,* she thought. She didn't think she could be rational enough to be brave if one of the bodies in that mausoleum was a baby. She told herself, before looking, that the cry, weak as it was, was from a real, living child, and *if* there was a dead baby listed, that would have to be just a coincidence.

But she thought herself lucky that none of the dates indicated a dead newborn.

She went back around to the front. She cupped her hand under the padlock and noticed for the first time that the shackle part had been cut.

It had to have been that way before, when they'd all been standing here looking in. Otherwise she would have heard the sound of someone sawing or cutting the lock.

Hmmm, Janelle thought, *a poor, frightened unwed teenage mother—with a pair of bolt cutters.*

She didn't open the doors but stood once again on her tiptoes. As before, at first everything was black, then shapes seemed to form out of the darkness: six coffins. With six dead people inside.

Something moved. Just barely visible in that almost nonexistent light, on the floor, toward the back corner on the right-hand side. Somehow they had all missed seeing it. It looked like a pile of rags. But it stirred. And the faint cry came again.

Janelle put her hand on one of the doors.

With a creak of metal on stone, the door pushed in, scraping the floor since—apparently—there had been some settling. A smell of musty old leaves tickled Janelle's nose. *Just leaves,* she tried to convince herself. *Just leaves.*

She stepped into the mausoleum, still unable to make out much of what lay on the floor in the back. It had to be a baby blanket, she supposed, though now that she was closer, and with the additional light from the open door, it looked more tweedy than a traditional baby blanket—and were those arms, like a coat?

And a string, a long string, was attached to the bundle and made it move even as she watched, leading from the bundle to—

The door slammed shut behind her, enclosing her in darkness.

Janelle whirled around and could make out the silhouette of someone standing between her and the door. Someone with long scraggly hair: the man they had seen before, by the fountain—looking, she hoped, too much like a stereotype of a bad person to actually be one. He made that sound, somewhere in between a kitten and a baby. Then he dropped his end of the string and he said, "Hey, little girl, wanna explore with *me*?"

She managed a paltry little squeak—hardly a scream at all—before the man clapped his hand over her mouth. He tasted of sweat and dirt. She tried to wiggle out of his grasp, but he held her tight. She kicked, she jabbed with her elbows, she bit, but—strong as she had always considered herself—he shoved her down to the floor as easily as though she were a five-year-old. Her head clunked against the stone and she lost a moment or two of consciousness.

The next thing she saw was the long, long knife in the man's hand.

"No!" she screamed the instant she realized he'd uncovered her mouth.

"'No,'" he mimicked her, and he made the crying-baby sound again as he moved the knife closer to her throat.

But then there was a screeching sound that she hoped, she prayed, was the door opening again. Somebody from her class must have noticed that she was no longer with them. *Let it be one of the boys,* she wished, and not Alycia who was only about four and a half feet tall—or, in fact, any of the other girls, or even Ms. Hurston. What she needed was defensive lineman Reid. But she'd settle for Brandon.

Except that the little room hadn't gotten lighter the way it had when she'd opened the door before.

It wasn't one of the doors opening.

It was one of the coffins.

Something poured out of the coffin. At first Janelle thought it looked like smoke, or fog, but in another moment it took on a definite shape, a man, except that his edges weren't very stable, and she could see through him. He wore a three-piece suit. And he hovered, his feet not quite touching the ground.

It was enough to—for a moment—actually make her forget the man with the knife.

This was a ghost.

She was actually seeing a ghost.

And then she heard a ghost.

"Well, look at this, Margaret," said the man who looked like a banker, except for the fact that little wisps of him kept getting caught in the draft. "I thought I smelled live people."

There was more screeching. The five other coffins opened.

From one of them arose a woman in an ivory-colored dress that reminded Janelle—who had been primed all day by Ms. Hurston to notice details—of the kinds of dresses she had seen in pictures in her history book, from between the two world wars. This woman said, "I don't know, Daddy. I do believe that one smells almost-one-of-us to me."

Janelle assumed that meant her. She assumed it meant she was about to die. She just didn't know if that would be from fright—could someone actually die from fright?—or from her attacker slitting her throat. She could only assume that he was offering her up to these dead people. She remembered the conversation on the bus—about the undead sucking the life force out of the living through their eyeballs. Apparently they couldn't do that. Apparently they needed a live person to lure someone here to be killed and to be made into one of them.

But her attacker jumped to his feet, letting the knife clatter to the stone floor. He didn't look as though he'd been expecting any of this. Perhaps the talking, moving dead people were a surprise to him, too. Looking as scared as she felt, he pulled the door open.

One of the other women—an old, old, grandmother—kicked the door shut before he could get out. "Nasty man," she called him.

"Nasty," echoed the third woman, who was wearing what appeared to be a wedding dress. "Freddy, Bobby—do something."

There were two other men with her, both wearing old-fashioned military uniforms, though one looked even more old-fashioned than the other. They floated away from the shelves toward the man who had lured her in here—apparently *not* because he was on friendly terms with them.

Her attacker tugged at the door, and though his hands passed right through the grandmother, who stood there looking fragile enough that it seemed a breeze would dissipate her, the door did not budge.

The man who looked like a banker said, "You, sir, are a disgrace. How dare you break into our home?"

When her attacker tried to beat the spirits away, his hands passed through them. But the spirits were able to hold on to him, and they dragged him away from the door.

So the ghosts *would* be able to kill her without any help from the living. Janelle very much hoped that it wouldn't hurt, that it wouldn't be—as her classmates had been joking—through having her life force sucked out via her face.

Instead, the grandmotherly one said to Janelle, "No damage done. Make wiser choices, young lady. But don't be afraid of us."

They *weren't* after her?

Janelle felt someone's solid hands support her as she got to her feet, and it was the older of the two military men. When she tried to grasp his hand to thank him, her fingers passed through him, though he smiled kindly.

Still, when she looked back from the doorway, the spirits were clustered around her attacker. Though all they did was crowd him, he was unable to catch his breath. He wheezed, he gasped, he fell to his knees.

"Go," the woman named Margaret urged her. "Run."

Janelle ran.

Out the door.

Across the gravestone-littered grass.

Down the hill.

Along the cemetery road until she caught up with Xavier and Courtney, who were straggling behind the rest of her classmates.

"Looks like it's going to rain," Xavier said mildly.

And she took a deep breath, and another, and another.

Then she said, without even checking the sky, "Probably."

She never did tell anybody what had almost happened.

And she most especially didn't tell what *had* happened.

Not even when she heard Mount Hope Cemetery mentioned on the news the next day. She learned that authorities—checking the cemetery after Halloween night to make sure no pranksters had caused any damage—had found a dead man in a crypt that had been broken into. Despite the large knife that was on the floor beside him, the man looked to have died by natural causes: He had simply stopped breathing. The police described him as a homeless man, and they speculated he had been using the crypt to sleep in, because they found his tattered tweed coat bundled up as though he'd been using it as a pillow.

Ms. Hurston, Janelle thought, would be appalled at the politically incorrect stereotyping.

The news report went on to say that there was no evidence the coffins had been disturbed.

"Fortunately," the report ended, "there was no damage done."

BEST FRIENDS

BEST FRIENDS

NIKKI

This is a picture of me and my best friend, Aimee Ann. We've known each other since kindergarten, when our mothers ran into each other—almost literally!— in the school parking lot. Afterward, while they were waiting for us, they got to talking and realized we lived only one block apart, which meant each of them could drop us off and pick us up half the time if they carpooled and took turns.

It was like Fate.

We were destined to be inseparable best friends.

Aimee Ann loves my mom just as much as I love hers. It's like we both have two families.

As kids, we used to share toys; now that we're teens, we've moved on to sharing makeup. On occasion we have been known (don't tell the teachers!) to share homework. We've always shared clothes. That's one of the main reasons to have a best friend! We once even shared a boyfriend—though that, honestly, was a bit of a test of our relationship. But then we figured you can get a boyfriend—especially one of Chuckie Zarpentine's quality—anywhere. But how often are you going to find a forever friend?! So we both dumped him.

This picture is from last summer. Every year for, like, the last five years, Aimee Ann's parents have rented an RV for a week at Darien Lake and—because they know better than to try to separate two best friends!—they invite me to go with them. Camping, swimming, enjoying all-week passes at the amusement park, being together day and night: It's like one, never-ending pajama party for two.

You can see the Ferris wheel in the background. Aimee Ann and I love riding on Ferris wheels.

Notice how we're wearing our matching Mickey Mouse T-shirts? "You're like twins," my mother said, then laughed, when she brought them home for us, "separated at birth."

Aimee Ann and I loved those T-shirts.

AIMEE ANN

I know I sound like a cold, hateful monster when I complain about Nikki.

But, oh, those retarded Mickey Mouse shirts. I don't think I ever truly hated an article of clothing as much as I hated those. I mean, c'mon, we were about to start *high school,* not third grade—and they were secondhand from the Volunteers of America Thrift Shop. The one Nikki gave me had some sort of anonymous stain on the front, like maybe the previous owner had a problem with getting her food into her mouth in any consistent manner, or maybe she just drooled a lot.

Nikki might or might not have noticed. She could be hard on clothes herself. She was always borrowing my stuff and returning it with stains or spills or snags or stretched-out waistbands.

But, "Be nice," my mother kept telling me. "The Bianchis haven't had as easy a life as we have. It wouldn't hurt you to be bighearted."

The Bianchis. Poor husbandless, friendless Mrs. Bianchi, who worked at the Stop 'n' Go Mini Mart in the afternoon and as a bartender in the evenings. Ever since they met, when she almost ran my mother down in the school parking lot (and any truly sane mother would have taken that as an omen), she and my mother were supposed to take turns driving us to and from school. But Mrs. Bianchi was always calling to say, "Could you please drive the girls in tomorrow? I'm having to work the late shift, and morning comes around so fast when I haven't gotten home till 3 A.M. I mean, I *could* do it if you can't . . ." Or, "I know it's my turn to pick the girls up, but I need to cover for one of the other cashiers, who didn't come in today . . ."

Even on days when she *said* she'd pick us up, Nikki's mother wasn't reliable. After she forgot us at school two or three times, my mother learned to hang around the house around two forty-five or three o'clock so I could call her, just in case.

Don't tell me Mrs. Bianchi didn't count on that.

"It's rough for her," my mother would defend her, "with no husband and having to work two jobs." She didn't seem to mind Mrs. Bianchi taking advantage of her, and she didn't seem to mind Nikki taking advantage of me.

And poor fatherless, friendless Nikki. Who only had me.

Not counting my parents, of course, who always took her side.

"Ooh, I've never seen such a beautiful doll," Nikki would say, and my mother would nudge me, hard, until I would say, "Oh well, I hardly ever play with her anymore. Would you like her?"

Nikki never turned down anything my mother forced me to offer to her, no matter how grudgingly I made that offer.

Or, "Ooh, that sweater is so soft. And it matches

perfectly the stripe in that skirt my mother just got me at the consignment shop. You're so lucky. It's tough to get matching pieces secondhand."

Always in front of my mother, Mrs. We-Must-Be-Aware-of-Our-Standing-and-Our-Obligations-in-the-Community. Mrs. Soft-Touch. Mrs. Easy-Mark.

Nikki always wanted to do whatever I was doing, be with who I was with. When we were younger, it was flattering, and I admit there was a certain fascination for me to be at the Bianchis, since Mrs. Bianchi believes the food pyramid consists of pizza, root beer, and chocolate, and in every other way, too, is just about as opposite my mother as two people can be. But after a while, Nikki became almost a stalker. She joined the choir just because I did, and the chess club, and the volleyball team. She'd ask to copy my homework; and if I didn't let her, it meant she'd get detention; and then I'd have to stay after, too, since we rode together, so what was the point of saying no?

Last year, after Chuckie Zarpentine and I had worked together for a week on our final joint economics report, then skated together for four couples-only numbers at Krista Orsini's roller-skating birthday party, and I was just waiting for him to invite me to the Last-Chance-Before-Summer Dance, Nikki went ahead and asked him to go with her. Like she hadn't heard me saying, "Oh, I hope he asks me," every time he walked by for about two months.

I refused to talk to her for a week, then she showed up at our house, crying and claiming she'd had no idea I'd been interested in Chuckie, offering to break up with him, and begging to be friends again.

Did my father, who may be brilliant as a tax auditor, a church alderman, and a world-class Scrabble master catch on that she apologized only *after* the dance?

That was when he invited her, yet again, to Darien Lake with us.

NIKKI

Now that I'm dead, I find myself kind of floating rather aimlessly.

If there are other dead people around, I'm not aware of them. And living people seem totally unaware of me.

The first person I tried to talk to after the accident was—of course—Aimee Ann, since she is, was, and always will be my best friend. I was sure if any two people could connect the world of the living with the world of the dead, it would be us.

Nothing.

I tried my mother, both before and after she was told of my death.

Nothing there, either.

I tried my deadbeat father.

No wonder my mother left the creep.

I even tried the guy who had run me over with his car.

What's the good of being a ghost if you can't even haunt the person who killed you on Halloween night?!

There's nothing—besides me—in the world of the dead. And in the world of the living, I can pass through walls, but I also pass through anything I try to pick up—unless I give it my absolute, total, don't-even-*think*-about-thinking-of-anything-else(!) concentration.

But I can be single-minded.

It's one of my best attributes.

I concentrated with all my being.

When a ghost tells you that, she is not speaking figuratively.

I concentrated with all my being, and—eventually—I was able to pick up this picture that my mother had tucked into the coffin with me.

I was able to take the picture out of my dead hands and up into my spirit hands.

I am bringing it to Aimee Ann to comfort her in her sorrow. To let her know that not even death can separate us.

AIMEE ANN

I didn't mean to kill Nikki.

We were walking home from Celeste Camillo's Halloween party because Mrs. Bianchi was supposed to pick us up, but—surprise!—she hadn't shown up. Meanwhile, my parents were at a tax auditors' Halloween party for my father's company (one can only imagine how much fun *that* was), and it was too embarrassing—half an hour after everyone else had left and Celeste was sitting on the couch yawning so hard her jaw was cracking—to ask her to roust her parents out of bed and drive us the few blocks to our houses.

Nikki was wearing an outfit that was supposed to make her look like a rock star, because that was what I had told her *I* was going as. But I've known Nikki for ten years, so I saw *that* coming, and all along I'd been planning on dressing like an Egyptian princess, which I'd seen in the window of a costume rental place. But when I showed it to my mother, she said it was too expensive and I could put together a princess costume from some of the fabrics she had stockpiled for projects she'd never gotten to.

Princess, of course, is totally different from *Egyptian princess,* but my mother pretended to be oblivious to the nuances.

So I went dressed as trailer-park trash, which meant, basically, I dressed like Nikki, which—I know, I know—was cruel, and I'm totally ashamed of myself. But in my own defense I can honestly say that anyone can always count on Nikki, also, to be oblivious to nuances.

I even wore the Mickey Mouse shirt, and my only excuse is that I was in a foul mood because of my mother's lack of Halloween spirit.

So there we were, walking home together at almost one o'clock in the morning, and Nikki was going on and on about what a great time we always have at Darien Lake.

She had pulled out of her purse that snapshot she carries everywhere and was telling me—yet again—how much alike we are. As if! She said, as she does each time she shows the picture to anyone, "My mother has to take my word for it which of us is which."

Yeah, right, Mrs. Bianchi. I'm the one with the pained expression because your daughter's got her arm around my neck in a stranglehold that would make the

World Wrestling Federation proud. I'm the one with the green complexion because no matter how many times I tell Nikki, "Nikki, I don't like Ferris wheels because I can't stand heights," she always insists that I got over my fear of heights last time and tells me what a really great time we had, and my parents say, "Oh, go on with her—rides are more fun for two than alone," and she drags me on, and I spend the next two hours feeling ready to puke.

So there we were on Halloween night, walking home in the cold and the dark, and I was thinking I probably should have peed before leaving Celeste's, and Nikki was chattering on and on and on about how great the Ferris wheel at Darien Lake is because it goes *so* high up you can see just about all of the park spread out below you.

"Nikki," I said, talking over her because when she gets on a roll she doesn't even stop to take a breath, "I hate Ferris wheels."

"No, you don't," she corrected me. "They're fun." She was walking on the edge of the curb, balancing herself like a tightrope walker. She said, "People need to get their adrenaline going once in a while. Ferris wheels are a good kind of scare."

"Like this?" I said. And I shoved her. I thought she'd totter on the curb, her adrenaline going.

In the darkest recesses of my heart, I even suspected that, taken unawares, she might fall off.

I never saw the car.

I never, *ever* saw that car.

And I'd give anything—anything—to take that moment back.

NIKKI

Of course I know Aimee Ann didn't want to hurt me. Best friends don't want to hurt each other!

That's why with total, absolute concentration I've worked so hard until I've been able to move the picture from my coffin to the stairs by her bedroom.

She'll bend down to see what it is, and she'll know I've forgiven her.

Then with total, absolute concentration, I'll push her.

And then I won't be alone anymore. We'll be together forever and always.

Just the way best friends are meant to be!

PRETENDING

The moon wasn't up yet, and out here in the country, the night was darker than it ever got in the city. Brian turned on the overhead light and glanced again at the directions to Kyla Zolla's house.

"She might have just said, Drive till you get to East Nowhere," he grumbled to himself, "then keep on driving till you run out of gas or fall off the edge of the earth, whichever comes second."

If he had looked at the directions during study hall, when she'd passed the note to him, he might have known to suggest that she get a family member to drive her to school for the Halloween dance. One should always be leery of a set of directions that includes county route numbers instead of street names, and that says things like, "Pass by the Feed and Tractor store, then turn right at the first *paved* road." And "If you get to the falling-down barn with the old sign that says GUTHRIE'S POULTRY, you've gone too far."

Sure enough, Brian saw the GUTHRIE'S POULTRY

sign. Sighing, he made a U-turn, hardly having to slow down at all since there was no other traffic in sight.

"This better be worth it," he muttered. He had to turn on the light again to see his watch. He hadn't figured out yet how to set the car's clock, which wasn't just off by the hour, like it was from a different time zone, but was wrong when it came to the minutes, too. The good thing about the car was that it was a red Camaro. Never mind that it was almost as old as Brian. Red Camaros are total chick magnets.

Seven thirty. He'd told Kyla he'd pick her up at a quarter after seven.

It was her own fault for living so far out in the sticks. Who'd have thought the school district extended this far into the wilderness?

Brian found the paved road and turned down it, his headlights sweeping over the stubble of the field. It was October 31, and in upstate New York, you couldn't count on there not being a killing frost by the end of October, so most of the farmers had finished their harvesting—reaping—whatever it was farmers did that meant the produce was all out of the fields and in those nice little containers at the supermarket.

Brian passed by the traffic sign that showed a curve in the road, almost missed the forty-five-miles-per-hour sign that was his next landmark, then turned into what appeared to be a narrow unpaved road—but which, if Kyla's directions could be trusted, was really a long, windy driveway.

Finally, he came to the house—saggy porch, mud-splattered old pickup of indeterminate color, propane tanks. Yup. He had arrived.

He seriously considered just tapping the horn, but since this was his first date with Kyla, he figured he'd better go to the door and ring the bell. When he'd been going out with Maranda, he'd once beeped for her, and her parents had been dead-set against him ever since.

You'd think, though, seeing as how he *was* late, that Kyla *might* have been waiting for him.

Brian got out of the car. He'd forgotten how cold it was. His breath smoked in the air as he climbed the porch stairs and rang the doorbell. If there wasn't at least a dusting of snow by morning, there would definitely be a frost.

The light went out in the window, which Brian hoped meant Kyla was about to come outside and not force him into a meeting with The Parents.

In the sky, a multitude of stars twinkled merrily but did nothing toward brightening the night.

Brian stamped his feet impatiently for warmth and

just barely restrained himself from muttering out loud, "C'mon, c'mon, c'mon."

The door opened slowly and with a squeak.

A woman and a man stood there. In the light of the candle she held, Brian saw she had waist-length dark hair, and she was dressed in a long, black gown; the guy had hair that was slicked back, and he was wearing a black tuxedo and a black cape with red satin lining. The man rested his hand on the doorjamb, showing fingers with long, clawlike nails.

Brian took a step backward, startled—he told himself—by the fact that they weren't Kyla, and not by their pale faces and their fangs.

"Velcome to our house," the man said in a thick accent from somewhere between Hollywood and Transylvania. "Come in and let us drink your blood."

From inside the house Kyla's voice called out, "Brian? Don't let my parents freak you out. They aren't usually this weird."

Also sporting an accent of some kind or another, Mrs. Zolla said in a throaty voice, "Trick or treat."

How. Totally. Lame.

"Um," Brian said. "Yeah."

Even Maranda's family, which included six or seven kids younger than Maranda, didn't go this overboard about Halloween.

"Vhere is your costume?" the man—Kyla's dad—demanded. Neither of them had made any move to invite Brian in off the porch. "Don't you know vhat night this is?"

Brian pointed to his T-shirt, which was black. Of course, he'd probably have worn the shirt even if it wasn't Halloween, but nobody else had to know that.

Kyla's parents stayed rooted in the doorway. "Ah," the mother said in her gravelly voice that sounded more Russian than Transylvanian, "he is wearing disguise of American teenage boy. Beneath disguise, he is fifty-two-year-old South American dictator."

Momentarily minus the accent, the father said, "He better not be if he expects to take *our* daughter out." He grinned, either to indicate he was joking or to show off his fangs. And he wiggled his clawed fingers on the doorjamb to make sure Brian noticed.

You can't hold people accountable for their dorky parents, Brian reminded himself. On the other hand, he was ready to get back into his car, when Kyla's voice called, "Mom? Don't let Dad scare him away. I'll be down in a minute, Bri."

He was only twenty minutes late. How silly of him to think she'd be ready.

"Bri?" Kyla called again. "Mom? Dad? You *have* invited him in out of the cold, haven't you?"

"Of course, dahlink," Mrs. Zolla said, stepping back.

Mr. Zolla stepped back also. "Ve vill keep him entertained before ve drink his blood," he called over his shoulder.

Wonderful, Brian thought. Life would be so much easier if girls came without parents.

Kyla said, "Well, don't drink too much of his blood. He needs to have enough energy to be able to dance. You okay, Brian?"

"Yeah," he assured her.

"Don't make him sit in the dark, Dad," Kyla said.

The father switched the lights back on. The living room was nicer than Brian would have expected from the outside. Big old heavy mahogany and walnut furniture that his mom, who loved antiques, would have drooled over.

From a table that was by the door, Kyla's mother picked up a silver tray that held candied and caramel apples. "Trick or treat," she repeated. Brian was just thinking that in the city you could never have Halloween treats that weren't wrapped and tamper-proof, when she added, "Ones on right-hand side are without razor blades or broken glass."

"And here I am, on a diet," Brian lied.

A set of stairs curved up to the second floor. Kyla

peeked her head around the corner. "Hi, Bri. Costume issue here. I'll be another minute."

"You know," Brian started, "I've been to these things before, and usually it's just the ninth graders and the dorkiest tenth graders who wear . . ."

But she'd ducked back into her room. All he'd seen of her was that she had her long blond hair pinned up on her head. He hoped, as long as she was going for a costume, that it would be a sexy outfit—more French maid, and less, for example, Humpty Dumpty. Last year, Maranda had gone as Tinker Bell and had wanted him to go as Peter Pan. "Yeah, right," he'd told her. He'd known before they started that it would be difficult enough to get her interested in making out when she was wearing wings and pixie dust; and he could only imagine how the night would have gone if he'd had to contend with that stupid hat and green tights.

Mrs. Zolla said, "I go up and help dahlink daughter."

While she went upstairs, Mr. Zolla, still sounding like the Count on *Sesame Street,* asked Brian, "May I get you something to drink?"

There was no telling how long a costume issue could take, so Brian said, "Sure," and followed him out into the kitchen.

The kitchen was large and very modern—white

paint and brushed stainless steel. Brian guessed it was too much to hope that he would get offered a beer. Mr. Zolla knew Brian went to high school with Kyla, no matter what the fake ID in his wallet said.

But when Mr. Zolla opened the refrigerator, which was one of those super-expensive ones with the flat-screen TV built into the door, the refrigerator was empty except for maybe a dozen of those bags like the Red Cross uses to collect blood.

"Ve have A, B, or O-negatiff," Mr. Zolla said.

This Halloween routine was wearing awfully thin. Even knowing that the dark red substance in the bags had to be some kind of fruit punch, Brian's stomach went queasy. "I think I'll pass," he said.

Mr. Zolla shrugged and took out a bag for himself. Using the tubing as a straw, he slurped a mouthful, then gave an appreciative *mmm*. Then, "No?" he asked Brian. "Sure?"

"Oh, yeah," Brian said. "I'm sure."

They went back into the living room just in time to hear someone climb up onto the porch.

Mr. and Mrs. Zolla would probably scare the pants off any young trick-or-treaters, Brian thought with a certain amount of anticipation. But the door opened without the doorbell having rung, and a young man walked in.

"Hey, Dad."

Had to be Kyla's older brother: His hair, though almost military-short, was the same color as hers, and he had her smile, which he flashed at Brian. "Hey, you must be the new boyfriend. Brian?" He offered his hand. "I'm Trevor."

Mr. Zolla was scowling at Trevor's Old Navy sweatshirt and jeans. "Vhere is costume?" he demanded.

"The night's still young," Trevor told him. "The moon isn't even out yet."

Mr. Zolla didn't look mollified, but Trevor wasn't paying attention to him. "Hey, that must be your Camaro out there," he said.

Brian was ready to accept a compliment about the vintage car, when Trevor finished, "Your back left tire looks awfully punky."

"Oh, no. I just bought those tires."

"Maybe you ran over a nail or some barbed wire coming up here." Trevor shook his head. "Country roads can be murder on tires. Here, let's go take a look."

Mr. Zolla held up his Red Cross bag. "Vant some blood, Trevor?" he asked. "O-negatiff, your favorite."

"Better save some for the party," Trevor said. "Leave the front door open so we can have some light in the driveway."

Party, Brian thought as he followed Trevor back

outside. Duh. Then it made a little more sense how done-up Mr. and Mrs. Zolla were. Because—now that he thought of it—how could there be many trick-or-treaters when farmhouses were so far apart?

Brian crouched down in the gravel next to Trevor. *Punky* was an understatement. The tire was *flat*.

Kyla better be something really special before he'd ever come out here again.

"Got a spare?" Trevor asked.

"One of those stupid doughnuts," Brian said. *That* would probably not last from here to the dance, back here, back home—never mind any potential side trips. *Besides* looking stupid, like a Loony Tunes tire.

"You know," Trevor said, "we can probably fix this one."

Brian looked at him skeptically.

"Country roads," Trevor reminded him. "If we had to go to a service station every time we ran over something sharp, we'd have had to sell the farm years ago."

Brian resisted the urge to ask, *And that would be a bad thing?*

"Can you jack it up and get the wheel off?" Trevor asked. "I'll fill a vat of water so we can dunk the tire and tell from the bubbles where the leak is. Then I can put a plug in, we put the tire back on, jack the car down, and you'll be all set to go. Who knows? By the time we're done, my sister might even actually be ready."

"Yeah, right." Brian snorted.

"I'll get set up in the barn," Trevor said.

Brian got the jack out of the trunk and had the lug nuts off and the car up before he realized that Trevor hadn't come back. He pulled the wheel off the axle, and still there was no sign of Trevor. Brian looked up the driveway to the barn and thought, *So much for what WE will do*. Despite the coldness of the night, he was hot from struggling with the wheel. It would have been nice for Trevor to reappear now so he could lend a hand. Brian checked the tire, but there was no obvious puncture.

Still no Trevor.

Brian set the wheel upright and tried to roll it up the driveway the couple hundred yards to the barn, but there was so little air in it, the tire kept catching on the flat side. Still, it would be wimpish to leave the tire here, go to the barn to fetch Trevor, and ask him to do the carrying.

Brian picked the tire up, knowing he was getting dirt and gravel on his hands as well as his black T-shirt.

He struggled his way to the barn and kicked open the door, then simultaneously let the tire drop. "Here we are," he said, with only the slightest emphasis on the "we."

No sign of Trevor.

There was a light on overhead, which illuminated bales of hay and all sorts of equipment that Brian, a city boy, didn't recognize. One whole section of the barn was set up like a workshop where, conceivably, someone could do stuff like, for example, plug a tire. But there was no tub of water, no Trevor.

"Trevor?" Brian called, thinking there were lots of places behind which Kyla's brother could have gone to fetch whatever it was he needed.

No answer.

It was eerily quiet out here. No traffic going by, no neighbors, no animals—beyond the hint in the air of a recently startled skunk. Didn't all farm families have at least a pet dog or cat or chicken?

"Trevor?"

Maybe the vat Kyla's brother had been looking for wasn't in the barn. Maybe he'd gone back into the house to see if it was there.

Except, of course, that then he would have passed by Brian.

Brian brushed the dirt off the front of his shirt and looked at his watch. Ten after eight.

Even if Trevor had gotten distracted and wandered

off, you'd think maybe *Kyla* might have been concerned enough to check up on her date.

"Trevor?" he called again, very loud this time.

Brian went outside. He *could* check around behind the barn, just in case Trevor had gone there. But he remembered what night this was, and he remembered how enthusiastic Trevor's parents were about Halloween, and—normal, reasonable, and friendly as Trevor had seemed—there was the chance that he might be waiting back there in the dark, ready to leap out at Brian, cause him to jump in fright. The story of Kyla's gutless boyfriend that the family had pranked would go down in the annals of Zolla family folklore to be repeated and laughed about at graduations, weddings, picnic reunions, and Halloween parties for years to come.

Halloween parties reminded him that guests were expected at the house.

No sign of any cars. Just his Camaro, sitting with its driver's side rear end sticking up in the air, bathed by the light from the still-open front door.

How late a start were they getting for this party?

Brian walked back to the house. Unless there was a prank going on that Mr. Zolla was in on, too, you'd think he might have had some curiosity about how his son was faring with changing his daughter's date's tire.

"Hello?" Brian called from the porch into the open doorway. He felt self-conscious about just walking in, but Mr. Zolla wasn't in the living room, and Brian wasn't going to wait outside in the cold and dark, with Trevor potentially looking out for the opportunity to shout "Boo!" at him.

Brian walked into the house.

"Hello," he called, thinking maybe Mr. Zolla was in the kitchen, hitting some more of that "O-negatiff."

The house was as quiet as the barn had been.

"Kyla!" Brian called from the foot of the stairs. *C'mon, c'mon, c'mon. Enough is enough.*

There was a *click!* behind him, and the Zolla family was just strange enough that—even as he whirled around—he found himself wondering if a secret door had opened. But there was no door, and in another moment the source of the click became evident as the big grandfather clock in the corner bonged the first quarter of the Westminster chimes melody.

It was a fancy old piece, massive, obviously hand-carved, with an impressive pendulum and weights, a dial to show the phases of the moon, and a clear but resonant tone.

A lot of money in this family.

Brian supposed that made them eccentric rather than nuts.

When the last echoes of the chimes had died away, Brian became aware of another sound, this time coming from the kitchen—a hissing, crackling sound.

"Trevor?" Brian called, not because he believed anymore that Trevor would ever answer, but because he felt funny walking through the house without announcing himself—just in case he ran into Mr. or Mrs. Zolla and they accused him of snooping. And of doing away with their son.

The lights were all still on in the huge, white kitchen. No one was there, but someone had put a pot on the stove. It was boiling over, which was the sound Brian had heard.

So they planned to serve their party guests something beyond blood-colored punch in Red Cross collection bags, after all. But then someone had lost track of what he or she was doing. It would serve them right if he just ignored the overflowing pot and let their dinner get ruined. But now that Brian had walked in here, he couldn't very well claim he hadn't heard it. He was sure somebody would come running in at any moment and catch him and berate him for being a fool who didn't know how to take care of boiling water.

Brian walked over to the stove and turned the heat off under the pot. The water was white with foam and continued to spill over the edge for another moment or two, sizzling on the still-hot burner. Even so, Brian considered it beyond his strictest responsibility to find a pot holder or a towel to move the pot onto a cold burner where it would cool down faster.

And still no sign of the Zollas.

Brian considered whether he should just fetch his tire from the barn, stick on the doughnut spare, and go home.

He glanced around the kitchen and saw there was a back door. Trevor could have gone from barn to house without passing him in the driveway—but why? Maybe he had been unable to find that vat for the water and had come in here to ask his dad where it was, and the two of them had gone down to the basement to look . . .

For fifteen minutes?

And all this while, Kyla and her mother were upstairs, oblivious to anything beyond hair, nails, clothes, and shoes?

Who knows? Brian thought. *Who cares?*

He was going to give her exactly one more minute, before he was out of here.

Watching the second hand on the wall clock made the time seem to pass even slower: the old watched-pot-never-boils syndrome. Brian glanced at the pot on the stove. The water had ceased bubbling, and Brian looked in, expecting to see pasta.

What he saw was a rat.

For a moment he hoped it was a rubber or plastic toy, but chunks of fur were floating on top of the water.

Brian backed away in revulsion. Clean as the kitchen looked, there must be rats in the walls; perhaps one had been walking along the back of the stove and fallen into the water.

Note to self: ABSOLUTELY, accept no snacks from the Zollas, here, or anything Kyla might ever bring to school.

And that, of course, was giving the Zollas the benefit of the doubt: that they hadn't been *cooking* the rat.

Brian left the kitchen without waiting for that full minute to be up. Enough was enough. He and Kyla were history.

In the living room, he paused.

Had he closed the front door behind himself when he'd come in?

He hadn't thought so.

But surely he would have heard if the wind had slammed the door shut.

Not that he had noticed any wind earlier.

Brian turned the doorknob.

Brian turned the knob the other way.

Brian tugged.

Brian fiddled with the locking mechanism.

He could hear it click, but no matter whether he had the switch to the right or to the left, the door did not budge.

And then, just when he was beginning to think maybe he should simply pick up a chair and fling it through the window to make his escape, he heard Kyla's voice from upstairs: "Brian? Is that you? Something goofy happened to the door to my room—and we're all stuck in here."

Brian was weighing her good looks against the option of ignoring her when Mrs. Zolla spoke up—without her accent: "Brian, before you come upstairs, can you check the kitchen? I put some water on to make deviled eggs, and it must be boiling over by now."

So. No rat soup planned for supper. That was a relief. And there was a reasonable explanation for where everybody had gotten to. The front door must simply be old and finicky: weather-stuck. Good thing no one had seen him overreact.

Since he'd already taken care of the boiling water, Brian headed for the stairs. "Which is your room?" he asked.

"First," the several family members answered simultaneously.

Brian admired the rich, curved staircase, the banister with carved wooden newels.

Nice house. Too bad about the family.

He opened the door, and a body fell out, a young woman with a bloody T-shirt and a knife sticking out of her back.

At the same moment Brian was registering that, the next door in the hallway opened, and there stood Kyla, Trevor, and Mr. and Mrs. Zolla.

So much for a sexy French maid costume—Kyla and her brother looked like younger versions of their parents. Dark hair. Pale faces. Clawed fingers. Vampires. They were all vampires.

And it was time to stop looking for a rational explanation for any of this.

"Quick!" Trevor called. "He's found the last victim! Don't let him get away!"

Brian spun around to run down the stairs, but his feet got tangled in the legs of the young woman who had fallen out of the closet. Rigor mortis must have set in, for she was positively stiff, and the next thing Brian knew, he was tumbling down the stairs.

He thought he'd reached the bottom—he was sure he had hit every single step on the way down—and he tried to stand up while he was still dizzy. Apparently, though, he hadn't been at the bottom after all, and he hit a couple more steps before coming to rest in a heap on the living room floor. He was sore all over, with his leg bent under him at an angle that was definitely scary.

Still, he began to crawl toward the door before he remembered that it was somehow sealed.

And that his car was minus a tire.

Behind him, he could hear footsteps clambering down the stairs. Someone was swearing, which—for a moment—he kind of thought might have been himself, but it was Trevor. And Kyla was giving frantic little gasps and crying, "Brian! Bri! Are you all right?"

He shrank away from the feel of hands on his shoulders, but they were gentle hands and when his eyes finally were able to focus, he saw that Kyla was kneeling in front of him, peering anxiously into his face. "Are you all right?" she demanded again, which was a strange thing for a vampire to ask. Then she said, "Here, give me that pillow."

Was she going to smother him?

No, she put the pillow, which her mother had whisked off the couch, between his head and the wall.

"Don't move him," Mr. Zolla said, having lost his accent also. "I'll call 911."

While Mr. Zolla picked up the phone in the living room and began telling someone that there had been a falling-down-the-stairs accident, Mrs. Zolla said to

Brian, "I'm so sorry. It was supposed to be a joke. Obviously it went too far. I'm so sorry. We never thought you'd fall down the stairs."

Brian cast a wary glance back up the landing, where the body still lay.

Trevor must have seen where he was looking. "It's a mannequin," he said. "From the costume rental place where I work."

Brian's leg was beginning to throb. Much as he wanted to believe . . .

"C'mon," Kyla said, "Bri. You know *I'm* not a vampire. I go to school with you. *During the day.*"

That was a good point.

But Brian couldn't tear his gaze off where the mannequin, or the body, lay. "The rat," he said, surprising himself at how slurred and unsteady his voice sounded. "The bags of blood."

"Brian," Kyla said in a tone somewhere between disbelief at how gullible he was and not wanting to chastise him since he was injured because of her—and her crazy family. "They're just novelties. My family *loves* Halloween. We go wild with the idea of pretending to be something we're not." She pulled the plastic fangs out of her mouth, took off her dark wig to reveal her pinned-up blond hair, ran the back of her hand across her pale cheek to smudge the makeup off her normal-colored skin, and peeled off the latex gloves that gave her fingers that look of claws.

Mr. Zolla was off the phone, and he crouched down beside Brian and shoved his Red Cross bag at him.

Brian shrank away from him, which meant leaning into Kyla, who—whatever was going on—was one of them.

"It's tomato juice mixed with cran-grape juice," Kyla's dad said. "Probably not a flavor that's going to catch on like wildfire, but it's certainly not real blood. Taste it."

Brian shook his head, unable to rid himself of the lingering fear that they wanted him to taste human blood because that would turn him into a vampire.

Mrs. Zolla must have gone out to the kitchen, because she was carrying the dripping rat on a slotted spoon. "It's just a plush toy," she said. "It's for cats to play with. Look."

Maybe. Brian couldn't bring himself to look that closely. His head was beginning to ache, and he thought he might become sick to his stomach. *Concussion,* he thought. *These nutcases have given me a concussion.*

Kyla took the Red Cross bag from her father and brought it closer to Brian's face. "*Smell* it," she insisted. She held it under his nose until he could hold his breath no longer.

He caught the unmistakable whiff of tomatoes.

"It was all a joke that went too far," Kyla said.

In another moment, he would allow himself to get angry, to let them know that he would encourage his parents to sue them right out of their pretty furnishings. But for now, he asked, "The flat tire?"

"That was me," Trevor admitted. "I let the air out. Not to worry: We've got a pump."

Brian shook his head, which was a mistake as far as his headache was concerned. "Why?" he asked.

"To keep you here till eight thirty," Kyla said.

"You might have asked," Brian grumbled. He was looking at the phone Mr. Zolla had been talking into and noticed that the cord was pulled out of the wall. He would ask about that in a moment, but for now he asked, "What's at eight thirty?"

"Moon comes up," Trevor explained.

"Full moon," Mrs. Zolla said.

"We're not vampires," Mr. Zolla started, and Kyla finished, "We're werewolves."

Brian was sure they were joking again . . .

Right up until the moment when he realized they weren't.

I WANT TO THANK YOU

Thank you.

Thank you so much for letting me in your house.

The townsfolk just seemed to suddenly go mad. It must be because it's All Hallows' Eve. There's no other reason for them to have decided I'm a witch and come after me. I didn't do anything.

Truly.

I'm a good girl. I always do what I'm told, and I never gossip about people or spread rumors.

So thank you from the bottom of my heart.

It was just coincidence that Mistress Charity fell down the same stairs she'd just been chastising me for not cleaning properly.

I have no powers. I have no evil in me.

I would never do her harm.

I would never do anyone harm.

Just like you. I can see the kindness in your eyes. That's why you let me in when I came running, running away from them, through the woods, and found myself on your doorstep.

I appreciate the protection you offered me when they banged on your front door and demanded you hand me over. Thank you for telling them you had never seen me.

You're obviously as kind a man as you are rich.

I see you have many fine things in your house. A man who surrounds himself with beauty must have a beautiful soul. And that's a good thing to know.

The people who accused me will be gone now. It's been hours and they must be far away now, searching elsewhere, or come to their senses.

I appreciate your hospitality. I appreciate your hiding me in this basement room where—even if they had forced themselves in—they would never have found me.

I am in your debt for your saving me from them.

I truly believe that this coffin you have down here is simply your way of looking ahead till the time—God grant many years from now—when you die.

I won't tell anyone.

Now please, please, please, let me go.

WHEN AND HOW

"I will tell you," the psychic said, "when and how you are going to die."

He paused to take a long drag on his cigarette, and Marissa's friends giggled and poked her in the back.

"Can you *do* that?" Marissa was surprised at the offer. She had thought this was the one question fortune-tellers shied away from. That was how this whole trip had started: Cara's mom had told them how the friend of someone she had once worked with had gone to a tarot reader who laid out the cards, turned pale, then said, "I can't do this," and returned the woman's money. Later that week, after going out to a downtown nightclub, Cara's mom's friend's friend had been attacked and killed in a parking garage.

The five of them, Marissa, Cara, JoLyn, Daphne, and Rodney—whom they liked to describe as the group's token male—hadn't been sure of the story. "Did that really happen?" Cara had asked her mom.

And though Cara's mom had assured them it had—a long time ago—with moms it was sometimes hard to tell these things for sure. It may well have been less a real incident than a warning against downtown or nightclubs or parking garages. Rodney had pointed out that many urban legends seemed like they might have gotten their starts as somebody's mom warning about something.

But Cara's mom's telling the story—in response to something Marissa could no longer even remember—had gotten the friends interested in going to Lily Dale, the psychic community in upstate New York, to get *their* fortunes told. What better way, they had decided, for five high school seniors to spend Halloween night, especially since they were too old for trick-or-treating, and too tall to bluff it, and the girls were all on diets, anyway. Rodney was not on a diet, as he had one of those metabolisms where he could eat anything without worrying about it ending up on his hips or butt, but he had given up trick-or-treating even earlier than the girls had, when his voice changed.

So off they went to Lily Dale.

This psychic had not been their first choice. They had stopped at several pretty little gingerbread Victorian houses in the community, which had signs picturing stars, or teacups, or tarot cards. But psychics were more expensive than the five of them had anticipated. Fifty dollars a session had been the going rate, no split sessions. They had already gotten back into Daphne's car—never mind they had driven two and a half hours to get here—when they noticed his tacky ranch house. On the front lawn was a sign that had a pair of penetrating eyes. No face—just the eyes. Either an optometrist or a psychic, and considering where they were, they guessed psychic. Since the house wasn't as nice as the others, they'd hoped his rate might be lower.

He was short and skinny and swarthy and stank of the cigarettes he chain-smoked, which were also short and skinny and dark—probably European. Apparently, Europeans hadn't heard that smoking was bad for you.

Fifty dollars a session, he'd told them—hadn't these people ever heard that price-fixing was illegal? But then he'd said that—if they preferred—for fifty dollars he would answer one question from each of them.

They could have gotten back into the car again—a five-hour-wasted round-trip—or they could go with Mr. Chain-Smoking-Euro-Man. Warily, they stepped into his house.

For someone who looked into the future, his decor definitely looked into the past. The 1970s, Marissa guessed from the orange-golden rug and the woodlike paneling of his dining room. But maybe she was being unfair. Maybe the paneling was expensive stuff, and it was just the coating from all the nicotine that gave it its dark, lusterless matte finish. Along with the anonymous stains on the tablecloth and the gray metal file cabinet in the corner, and the fact that he had only one dining room chair and had pulled five folding chairs out of the closet for them, the decor did not inspire confidence.

So now Marissa—faced with a prediction regarding the when and how of her mortality—asked, "Can you *do* that?" with a slight hope that maybe her question would bring the psychic back to his senses. "Oh," he would say, "what's the matter with me? I forgot: That's not allowed. Let me predict something else." Then she wouldn't have to say, "I'm not sure I want to hear this," and have the others laugh at her.

The psychic took another long drag on his cigarette and asked, "Can I do that? Is *that* your question, then?"

What a creep.

"No," Marissa said, "that was *not* my question." Despite the anticipation of coming, despite the long drive to get here and the disappointment when it had appeared they wouldn't be able to find an affordable fortune-teller, despite Cara and Rodney and Daphne and JoLyn going first, she had not had a question in mind, and the death thing had been the psychic's suggestion. Still, it was an unsettling topic. She wanted to answer: "I only want to know when I'm going to die if it's going to be at least twenty years from now. Otherwise, tell me if I'm going to get accepted at one of the colleges where I applied." That was pretty close to the question Daphne had asked, and everyone had called it lame, but Marissa didn't think she was up to hearing something like: A serial killer will get you within a week.

Still, she supposed the psychic already considered himself generous for not automatically answering and charging her for that dumb "Can you do that?" question and would not give any unpaid-for hints.

"So"—the psychic held the foul cigarette pinched between his fingers and inhaled as though his lungs were in his toes—"I will tell you when and how you will die."

Marissa took a steadying breath.

"It will be just over fifty-six years from now, four months short of your seventy-fourth birthday."

Marissa stored those figures in her head to work out when she had a couple moments to herself—to see if he'd guessed her age correctly, since he had not asked. It would be easier to trust a psychic who had not only the ability to zero in on a person's age but also demonstrated good math skills. In any case, fifty-six years from now was a much better number than, say, next week.

"You will die," the psychic continued, "in a plane

crash, while traveling from Rochester, New York, to Buffalo."

"Okay," Marissa said, slowly. She had never been on a plane, her grandparents all living within driving distance, and her parents believing in local vacationing. She figured if she hadn't flown anywhere in her seventeen years so far, she shouldn't miss skipping it later on. Besides that, she couldn't think of any reason she'd want to go to Buffalo. If this changed later in her life, Buffalo was only about an hour's drive away from Rochester. What kind of idiot would pay for a plane and spend more time going through airport security than it would take to drive where she wanted to go? She could readily arrange her life to exclude planes—and, in fact, Buffalo.

The psychic said, "I am not finished." He paused to take another toe-curling inhalation of his cigarette. "Your plane will crash in a sod farm in Batavia, New York, due to mechanical failure, sometime between 8:15 and 8:25 A.M., killing all aboard."

JoLyn poked Marissa and observed, "I can't imagine you being up early enough to catch an eight o'clock plane."

Easy for her to scoff: Marissa fully intended to add Batavia to her list of things to avoid once she hit her seventies, just in case the psychic meant that the plane would crash *on* her rather than with her *in* it.

"So," Rodney said, "all Marissa has to do is avoid getting on a plane when she's seventy-three, and she'll miss her appointment with death and live forever. Sweet deal."

That was pretty close to Marissa's reasoning, but the psychic was wearing a self-satisfied smirk.

Daphne told Rodney, "Living till you're seventy-three *is* living forever."

"I wish I'd asked when *I* was going to die," Cara grumbled. She'd asked if she'd marry Bailey Leonard, and the psychic had simply said no—which was what Marissa would have guessed in any case, Cara's boyfriend being very obviously not as much in love with Cara as Cara was with him. Obvious to everyone but Cara, for whom the negative had come as a surprise. She had asked, "Well, who, then?" but the psychic had said that was another question, and if she really wanted an answer, the group would have to buy another round of questions—for (of course) fifty dollars.

While Cara had still been considering, Rodney had asked, "Who will *I* marry?"

Marissa had always suspected that Rodney had a

bit of a crush on Cara—though Daphne maintained Marissa was a hopeless romantic and that *none* of the girls was or could ever be Rodney's type. Still, Marissa thought maybe he'd asked in the hope that the psychic would tell him he'd marry Cara.

But the psychic had told him he would not marry at all—which had caused Daphne to arch her eyebrows at Marissa.

Daphne, who was *not* a romantic, asked whether she would be accepted at Stanford, and the psychic had said yes, and that her acceptance would be in her mailbox Monday.

Marissa liked that this prediction would either come true or not in three days, which would give the rest of them a hint as to the psychic's accuracy, but JoLyn called it a waste of a good prediction. She asked, "Will I lead a happy life?"

"Happiness is subjective," the psychic had said, which had caused a howl of protest from all of them. It was hard to say whether the man had planned to leave the prediction at that, but after their outburst of catcalls and, "Not fair," and "Come *on*," he asked JoLyn, "Are you happy now?"

"Yeah," JoLyn had said. "Sure."

"You will never," the psychic told her, "be less happy than you are now."

So that had been the one unequivocally good fortune. Though Daphne at Stanford wasn't bad.

Now the psychic asked Cara, or maybe them all, "Do you have any further questions?"

Cara shook her head, and so did the others.

The psychic stood, which apparently meant they weren't going to be offered a Halloween candy bar or a glass of water or an opportunity to use the bathroom, or even a "Good-bye, it's been fun."

This—or the fact that it had gotten cold and started raining—put Rodney in a bad mood, and as he stepped out the front door he muttered, "I can tell fortunes, too: Smoking'll kill you."

Hard to tell if Rodney meant the comment for them or for the psychic, but the psychic *did* hear. He said, quietly and without emotion, "Yes," then closed the door firmly behind them.

They lingered under the overhang that someone with more ambition than this particular psychic might have tried to make into a patio. At seven o'clock, the night was dark, and the rain was pouring. Their breaths condensed in the cold.

"I hate driving in the rain at night," Daphne said. "It makes me nervous."

"Hey, I'm relaxed," Marissa said. "I don't know about the rest of you—but I know I'm safe."

"You're also not legal," JoLyn said, lording it over them just because she and Daphne had already had their birthdays and could drive at night. She took the car keys from Daphne. "And you all know you're safe with me, because I would not be happy if I had an accident. And you have all heard it . . ."—she shouted for the entire Lily Dale community to hear—"*I am destined to be happy.*"

Cara muttered, loud enough for JoLyn to hear, which meant she wasn't serious, "If you're destined to drive, then I'm destined to be scared."

Rodney said, "If we don't get out of here soon, we'll be destined to need an ark instead of a car."

So, screaming as though they were melting, they ran to the car, JoLyn and Marissa in the front seats, Rodney sitting between Daphne and Cara in the back.

The rain came down so hard, the windshield wipers—even on at maximum—had a difficult time keeping the windshield clear. The raindrops were fat and verging on being sleet. The fact that the streetlights reflected and glared on the wet pavement made Marissa glad she wasn't driving.

But JoLyn was confident and was doing a fine job. She had gotten them singing Christmas carols—since they couldn't find any decent radio stations, being still too far from Rochester, and since they didn't know any Halloween songs.

Rodney had started, "Up on the Housetop," but he didn't really know the lyrics beyond that, and he was floundering. After checking that the road ahead of them was clear, JoLyn, still gripping the steering wheel, glanced over her shoulder into the backseat as she energetically sang the refrain, "Ho! Ho! Ho! Who wouldn't go?"

In the front seat, Marissa saw the eighteen-wheeler ahead of them lose control on the slick road and begin to veer, then twist till it was sliding forward sideways, with their car aimed right at it.

There seemed to be all the time in the world for her to tell JoLyn to look out, to step on the brake—but carefully so that they wouldn't skid, too. There seemed all the time in the world to slow down safely. But it must have been only a moment, for JoLyn, all unaware, was still preoccupied with Rodney, was still belting out the second, "Ho! Ho! Ho!"

And then they hit the truck.

Just over fifty-six years later, four months short of Marissa's seventy-fourth birthday, the staff at Hillcrest

Home were discussing what to do with the old woman who had been in a coma ever since the car accident that had scrambled her brain and killed her four friends.

As far as they could tell, she had no family, or at least no one had come to visit in the two decades the most senior of them had been working there. For some reason, Hillcrest in Rochester was overcrowded, while their sister facility had several empty beds.

Since no one ever came to look in on her, and since she didn't know where she was, everyone agreed there could be no harm in sending her by air ambulance to Buffalo. A nice, short, safe trip.

WHEN MY PARENTS COME
TO VISIT

"**W**hen your parents get here, Matt," Nona tells me, "try to relax. Try not to let them get to you."

"You, too," I say by way of encouragement.

Yeah, right. Easier said than done. We both know that each of us will be ready to run from the room, screaming, before the night is done.

Not that running from the room, screaming, will help.

Which each of us knows so well that we both jump when the doorbell rings. Even though my parents never ring the bell. They just walk into my grandmother's house and start to spread cheer—spread it like an oil spill or a fungal infection.

I glance at the wall clock on my way to the door. Eight fifty-five. This is early for my parents—my father, VP of Marketing for a big insurance firm, and my mother, the attorney, who announced when she was still in high school that she was going to become the youngest female judge in the city. But it's kind of late for trick-or-treaters—especially since I turned off the light by the front door about half an hour earlier.

My parents always arrive promptly at nine o'clock. My father likes to say they're punctual. I like to say they're anal-retentive.

I open the door and find a group of four kids: two guys and two girls. They look about my age, which is fifteen, which is way too old to be going door to door, extorting goodies from the neighbors, even if you like Halloween.

I, personally, hate Halloween.

Although they are dressed in just regular clothes— jeans and sweatshirts—one of the girls wears a set of wings, which I guess she figures qualifies as an angel, butterfly, or bumblebee costume, and the other girl has a witch hat with a sparse fringe of fluorescent green hair overlaying her own blond hair. One of the guys wears a football jersey, which may or may not be a costume, and the other has a T-shirt with I BELIEVE MICHAEL JACKSON IS INNOCENT on it, which *has* to be a costume, because nobody really believes Michael Jackson is innocent.

They may well be classmates of mine, but my grandmother and I have just moved into this house in August and I don't yet know very many people in the neighborhood or in the school.

I am reaching into the bowl of Halloween-sized candy to give them each a handful—you don't want to tick off the kind of teenagers who're too old for trick-or-treating but who go trick-or-treating, anyway—when the angel/butterfly/bumblebee rattles a canister at me and announces, "Trick or treat for Unicef."

I keep to myself my doubts whether my donation will ever make it to Unicef, and I give them the money my grandmother gave me this morning to buy lunch in the school cafeteria. I had been so roiled up, knowing my parents were coming this evening, that I'd been unable to eat.

I give the four of them suckers, too, just in case they *are* from my school, even though none of them seem to recognize me any better than I recognize them.

When I close the door on the teenagers, Nona has come up behind me and she says, "You're a good boy, Matt," and she tousles my hair like I'm not a full head taller than she is.

"And you're a good Nona, Nona," I tell her.

"So where did Barry and Linda come from?" she asks with a sigh. Barry is my dad, Nona's son, and Linda, of course, is my mom.

We haven't even made it back into the living room when we hear them coming in. I'm about to glance at the clock, when I hear it start to chime. Nine o'clock, of course. Punctual, as always. And bickering and complaining as they come in, also as always.

"Ugly green," Dad comments to Mom about the color in the entryway. "It's reminiscent of that awful dress you wore at Seth and Nina's wedding, the shapeless one that made you look like a gigantic breath mint."

He is impeccably dressed in a charcoal-gray suit.

Mom has an ivory-colored skirt and jacket—business chic.

Apparently for this visit they have cast themselves in the role of style police.

"That was a lovely shade of green," Mom says, "and it couldn't have been *that* shapeless, because your so-called buddy, Leonard, spent the entire meal trying to look down my neckline while you were busy being tacky trying to sell life insurance to the other people at our table." She waves her arm to indicate the front hall. "But you're right: *This* is ugly mint green. Totally different from my daiquiri-ice-colored dress."

Fifteen seconds into the visit, and Nona is holding the bridge of her nose as though she has a headache already. "Hello, Barry. Hello, Linda. Are we going to try to make it through this visit without killing each other?"

Dad gives his mother an air kiss in the vicinity of her cheek. Mom acts as though Nona isn't even there.

I suspect her agreeing with Dad that the front hall is an ugly color will be her only concession to him tonight. "Hello, my little sweetums," she coos as though she hasn't noticed that I'm no longer six years old. She takes my hands, and her touch is cold and sends a shiver up my spine as she leans in to kiss my cheek. "Were those your friends, just leaving?" she asks. "Those girls looked hard and cheap. You could do better, handsome boy like you."

"They were just trick-or-treaters," I say. Maybe I mumble a bit, because my parents intimidate me.

My father says, "Stop mumbling. Stand up straight."

"He's not mumbling," Mom says. "Obviously there's something wrong with your hearing. Just like there's something wrong with your eyes: shapeless mint-green dress. Stop criticizing all the time. Do you want him to grow up mean, like your cousin Donald?"

"No," Dad counters, "but I don't want him to look and sound like an effeminate little pansy like your brother, Warren, either."

Mom gives a squeal of protest, but before she can say anything in defense of Uncle Warren, Nona stamps her foot. "Stop, stop, stop!" she shouts.

I try to escape down the hall and into the kitchen, but they follow me.

They always follow me.

"Come on," Dad says, "let's try to make this visit pleasant, for a change."

"You're the one who started it," Mom tells him.

I look at the clock on the stove.

They've been here for something like two minutes and already I feel like I'm about to throw up from anxiety, the way I did two years ago.

They followed me into the bathroom that time and made negative comments, based on my vomit, about what my grandmother feeds me.

At least moving into the kitchen sidetracks them from our relatives and from the dress my mother wore to her cousin's wedding ten years ago. This is the first time my parents have been to this house, and there are all sorts of fresh things to criticize.

"Butcher-block counters." Mom sniffs. "I didn't think anybody actually *did* butcher-block counters anymore."

"Please," I beg. "Is critiquing Grandma's decor really why you came?"

"Of course not, darling." Mom's fingers brush my cheek. "We came to see you. To make sure your grandmother is doing a good job of raising you—"

"—and not turning you into a pansy, like Warren," Dad finishes.

"I'm doing well in school," I say, to change the subject.

But it's a bad change.

Dad wants to know exactly what I mean by "well," and apparently B minus in most of my subjects doesn't count as "well." Of course he zeros in on the C minus in geometry. "Math is important," he lectures me, though I don't ask him how—ever—geometry has enhanced his life. The A that I've gotten in literature doesn't impress him. "Literature would be . . . like, what?" he demands.

"This particular unit is on poetry," I admit.

He smacks the palm of his hand against his forehead and proclaims, "Poetry is definitely for sissies. I don't know why these female teachers always try to emasculate—"

"Neanderthal woman-hater," Mom spits out at him.

Nona interrupts, saying, "You're here to visit Matt. How do you think this bickering and name-calling are making him feel?"

That calms them down for about another minute or so.

"So those weren't your friends?" Mom asks, going back to the kids they saw as they were coming in. "Don't you have any friends?"

My father says, "I hate overage hoodlums who go around on Halloween without even the pretense of a costume."

"They were collecting for Unicef," I say.

"Yeah, right."

It's the same thing I thought, but it sounds so petty and mean-spirited when he says it.

"Why *don't* you have any friends?" Mom asks.

"I didn't say I don't have any friends," I protest. "I just said *those guys* weren't my friends." Of course, I don't have many friends, as my grandmother and I move around a lot, but I hate how Mom has jumped to that conclusion.

"You belong to a team yet?" Dad asks, poking a finger at my chest. "You look kind of puny."

Mom slaps his hand down. "He does not."

"Track and field," Nona announces proudly.

"Like running and jumping?" Dad's tone clearly shows he's thinking *skipping and hopping.* "Oh, man. You need to try out for football," he tells me. "Put some meat on you."

"Oh, here we go again," Mom says. "Let's relive those glory days of yours—when men were men, and girls all carried pom-poms." She claps her hands, cheerleader-style. "Give me an *S.* Give me a *T.* Give me a

U-P-I-D. How pathetic that you peaked in high school."

"Yeah? And you never did peak."

"Barry," Nona warns.

Earlier, Nona and I brainstormed for topics to use to try to deflect them from sniping at each other, but my parents have a way of making my mind go blank.

Dad says, "You just sat around the house letting your butt grow to legendary size."

Mom squeals and puts her hands on her rear end. "I wear the same size now I did when I was in high school."

"Same size," Dad agrees, "but *a lot* more stress on those seams."

Mom glances around the kitchen, obviously looking for something to throw.

It was a mistake for me to come in here.

"Yeah?" Mom demands. "Yeah?"

Nona recommends to Mom, "Why don't you just take the high road and ignore him? Visit with Matt. You only have another"—she glances at the clock—"two hours and fifty-three minutes."

Is that all? It could just as well be two hundred and fifty-three years.

Of course, Mom doesn't want to take the high road

and ignore Dad. *High road* and *ignore Dad* are not in Mom's vocabulary. She tells Dad, "Well, all your fat's between your ears."

"Anybody want to hear my essay on why there'll never be peace in the Middle East?" I ask.

"No," Mom and Dad say simultaneously.

Peace in the Middle East? What about peace when my parents come to visit?

"Shrew," Dad calls Mom.

"Cretin," Mom retaliates.

We are never going to make it to midnight.

I try to slip inconspicuously out of the kitchen, to get away from all those knives that could be used as weapons, but my parents notice and follow me into the living room.

Nona says, "Do you see Matt's trophy?"

If I could have gotten her attention I would have signaled her *not* to mention the trophy.

Dad reads the plaque, then snorts. "Participation award. Participation award in track and field."

"It's good to participate," Mom says. "What is it with you that you think someone always has to grind somebody else's face in the turf and be declared"—she gestures quotation marks in the air—"'The Winner.'"

"Because that's better," Dad says, "than being"—

he makes quotation marks of his own—"'The Participator.'"

Rather than defend me, Mom says, "Oh, here we go. This sounds like an introduction for the long, boring story about running fifty-seven miles for the winning touchdown."

"Fifty-three," Dad corrects, "*yards.*"

"You sure it wasn't miles? End zone and back? In the snow? Uphill both ways?"

"Maybe you can brag on the time you got your nails done," Dad suggests. He holds his hands out and flips his wrists and—in a breathless falsetto—he says, "Aren't they just gorgeous? My hairdresser, Antonio, assures me, this *is* the color of the moment."

Nona is saying, "Who cares? What's it matter?" but this time my mother can't contain herself. She has to throw something at my father. She picks up my trophy and flings it.

He sidesteps and the trophy knocks the clock off the mantle.

I don't think either of them notices that both clock and trophy land in pieces. So much for my one and only trophy—even if it *was* just for participating.

"Beast!" she calls him.

"Psycho witch!"

"We wouldn't even be in this situation if it wasn't for you!"

"Me? You started it."

"Yeah?"

"Yeah."

"Yeah?" Mom launches herself at Dad, ready to use her nails on his face.

He grabs her wrists, but the force of her attack makes him take a step back and he trips over a stool. Still holding Mom, Dad staggers backward into the antique tea cart, where my grandmother has a bunch of her plants. Cart, plants, Mom, Dad—all crash onto the rose-colored rug.

The first few times this sort of thing happened, I tried desperately to get them to stop.

Now I worry about Grandma's rug.

I can smell the crushed greenery and the rich, loamy smell of the potting soil my grandmother has so lovingly used.

Mom catches hold of one of the plants. I don't know what it is: something stalky and sturdy. She swings it—ceramic-pot-end first—at Dad's head. The pot cracks from the impact with Dad's skull, showering dirt and leaves halfway across the living room.

"Stop it!" Nona shouts. "Can't you see what you're doing? Can't you ever learn?"

I don't say anything. They *can't* see. They'll never learn. What's the use?

Mom stands up, tottering a bit on her high heels.

Dad has dirt in his hair and blood running down the left side of his face; but before Mom can get away, Dad manages to catch hold of her ankle.

Mom pitches forward, arms flailing, taking the floor lamp down with her. The glass column part shatters, the shade snaps off and bounces, to land at my feet.

I pick up the shade and see the bottom rim is dented in. I concentrate on getting it straight without ripping the fabric while my father puts his hands around my mother's neck and squeezes.

Nona runs into the kitchen, fills a bowl with water, then comes back in to fling that water at my parents. I've heard this sometimes works with dogs or cats, but it has no effect on my parents.

By the time I have the shade looking as good as it will ever again look, my parents have begun to fade— almost as though the water has washed away their substance, but that isn't it. This happens every year. Sometimes Mom finds something to stab Dad with, once Dad pushed Mom down the stairs, another time—in an apartment my grandmother had that had a real, working fireplace—he pushed her into the fire, though she managed to hold on to him.

That was the worst.

Sometimes he starts the violence, sometimes she does, but it always ends the same.

"Damn," Nona says as they grow fainter and fainter, then disappear entirely, "and I had such hopes for this year."

Of course, she says that every year.

Nona sighs. "You'd think that having killed themselves once would have been one of those lessons with sticking power."

I was there that first time, too. I was only six at the time, and we'd been in the car, driving home from a Halloween party at the house of my father's boss. The party had been mostly for adults, but the boss had two kids that Dad had coached me on being nice to: a boy a year or two younger than me, who whined continually and smelled liked he wasn't thoroughly potty trained, and a girl a year or two older, who figured *she* was *my* boss. I'd had a terrible time, not to mention that it was way beyond my regular bedtime.

Apparently my parents hadn't enjoyed themselves any better than I had, though they didn't have that beyond-their-bedtime excuse. They squabbled and criticized, and each found fault with everything the other said until my mother took her can of hair spray out of her purse and squirted it into Dad's face.

I have no idea what she hoped to gain from that.

And I have to say that, even at six years old, I thought if Dad had spent more time trying to regain control of the car rather than—still—screaming at Mom that she was an idiot, we might not have hit that bridge embankment.

My parents were killed.

The only thing that saved me was being in my booster seat in the back.

My grandmother took me in and has been raising me ever since, which is mostly fine except that my parents come to visit every Halloween.

Nona thinks that if we could get them to refrain from killing each other until midnight—until the day after they died—that would break the cycle and they'd stop coming.

But it's a long time between nine and midnight.

"What a mess, what a mess," Nona sighs, her feet squishing in the puddle from the water she threw at them. She picks up the overturned tea cart. Some of the plants have come right out of their pots, and during Mom and Dad's struggle, they ground the dirt into the wet rug, which I'm guessing will probably never be the same again. Still, I get out the dustpan and start to sweep up the biggest chunks of dirt, plant, broken lamp, clock innards, and trophy bits.

"Next year," Nona says, "you'll have to try having some of your school projects in the front room, ready to show them. Just keep on talking, even if they criticize . . ." She corrects that to: "Even *when* they criticize. Try to just keep talking right over them."

"Okay," I say, not really believing it will work. Not really believing anything will work. Several years ago we hoped, my grandmother and I, that we could do that old trick—moving without leaving a forwarding address—but everybody showed up just as scheduled.

Nona must be able to read my discouragement in my voice. "You poor dear," she says. "You know your parents love you."

"Yeah, right."

"That's part of what keeps them tied to this night, coming back, despite all the harping they do on you. They want what's best for you."

Before I can say, "Then they should stop coming to visit," she finishes, "They just don't know what *best* is, and they don't know how to show it."

"Yeah," I agree, because it's what she wants to hear.

"I love you, too," she says. "And so does your grandmother, even though she can't stand to come down here to be with you."

"Yeah," I say again.

Nona stands on her tiptoes to kiss me on the forehead.

I'm already able to see through her, too, even though it isn't midnight, and she didn't die on Halloween. She died the year after my parents' accident, of a stroke. She isn't tied to Halloween but comes back to try to help me.

From the upstairs bedroom, Grandma Jean—my mother's mother—calls, "Are they gone yet, Matt?"

"Yup," I say as Nona disappears into the air.

"Go on up to bed," Grandma Jean says. "We'll clean the mess tomorrow."

EDWARD, LOST AND FAR FROM HOME

VIVIAN VANDE VELDE

"**A**ll Hallows' Eve," the old man said.

Edward, who had been rethatching the roof of the cottage, prickled and itched all over, and his hands were blistered from tossing pitchforks full of fresh bundles of straw onto the roof and then arranging them. He had just climbed down, finally finished with the task, and now he rested the pitchfork against the side of the cottage and gingerly opened and closed his fingers, knowing that—as much as they hurt now—they would hurt worse tomorrow.

"Yeah?" he asked warily.

The old man rarely spoke, and yet he had already called this information out once before, while Edward had been on the roof.

Because Edward had learned to read the old man's face—despite the overlapping wrinkles and pits from smallpox and the leathery quality that comes from spending one's life outdoors—he caught the glitter of annoyance and almost ducked in time. The old man's fist caught Edward on the ear.

"All Hallows' Eve!" he shouted as though Edward was hard of hearing. Edward wasn't hard of hearing— or at least he hadn't been before the old man had taken to cuffing him on the ear. He did sometimes have trouble understanding the old man's peasant accent, which was made even more indistinguishable because the old man's teeth were rotten stubs, so that his words whistled as well as stank; but luckily the old man rarely grunted more than three or four words at a time.

"All Hallows' Eve," Edward shouted back, to indicate he'd heard and understood.

The old man swung again, and this time Edward was able to back out of his range.

"Witches' sabbat," the old man said.

Edward held his arms out helplessly.

The old man gestured toward the pen where the two goats and the three sheep and the pig waited for their evening feeding. The old man must have been getting better at reading Edward's face, too. Or he had no confidence Edward had the wit to understand. He made an exaggerated gesture from the animals to the doorway of the cottage.

Oh. Indoors. He wanted the animals indoors, so

the witches wouldn't get them. With the roof newly mended, the stink would be held in nicely.

"All right," Edward said. Then, because he wasn't sure the old man understood and because he was afraid of the old man's fists, he said, "Yes. Indoors. I understand."

The old man walked away, shaking his head and muttering. Edward had no idea what he had said or done that the old man could have found fault with. He worked from sunup to sundown, backbreaking labor tending the fields and the animals and the house. His body was sore; his belly was never full; dirt had ground so deeply under his nails and into the creases of his skin, he doubted he would ever come clean again. His clothes were rags, and since the old woman had died in the heat of summer, fevered and coughing up a bloody flux, Edward had no idea where new clothes would come from, now that her loom stood idle.

Thinking of the old woman, Edward's mind skittered to the past winter, when his hands had gotten so red and raw from the cold, his skin had grown thin and cracked, and every movement brought pain. He had cried—he couldn't help himself—and the old man had kicked him for his noise. The old woman had given him a piece of raw wool from one of the sheep.

Edward had looked at it helplessly, having no idea what he was supposed to do with it. He had assumed she wanted him to draw it out into thread, the way she did. But the woman had taken it back into her own hands and rubbed it, not gently, onto his skin. He had jerked back in pain, but then his skin felt better, and he realized there was something in the wool that soothed all those tiny wounds.

It was the only bit of kindness he had experienced from either one of them.

The old man was nailing the shutters closed—against the witches, Edward supposed. The thought of witches made Edward shiver. The sun was low in the sky, the cloud tips touched by pink. It would be a cold night, and Edward guessed that he would probably be more grateful for the warmth of the animals indoors than he would be oppressed by their smell.

But still . . .

He didn't think he could survive another winter here, just him and the old man.

He had thought of running away, but there was no place to run to. He had gone with the old couple to the town for the Saint Bartholomew's Day Fair, and he had seen beggars there, and realized he had it hard, but not so hard as they. And he had seen a man with only one hand, a bloody rag wrapped around the stump, and another man with a brand on his cheek. For each of them the old woman had turned to Edward and said, "Thief."

It was a warning, he guessed. It was her way of telling him he was lucky they had taken him in at all, of letting him know that if he left—now that they'd fed him, more or less, and mended his clothes, more or less, and kept him alive, more or less—he owed them and they would have the right to come after him if he tried running away.

Or maybe she wasn't saying that he was legally beholden to them; maybe she was just reminding him that, being the useless fool he was, his two options were to rely on their charity or to thieve.

The old man had finished nailing the shutters closed, a job that was obviously too important to leave to Edward, who never seemed to do anything to the old man's satisfaction. Probably tomorrow he could be trusted to pull the nails out, and then he would have to hammer them straight so they could be used again for something else, since nails, even bent rusty nails, were too precious to be squandered. No doubt Edward would not hammer them out straight enough. Either that or he would spend too much time working on them. There would be *something* the old man would use as an excuse to strike Edward again.

Busy thinking about all this, Edward was slow to realize the old man was coming toward him, and here he was, having stood idle for the whole length of time it had taken the old man to hammer in four nails. Edward took hold of the pitchfork to return it to its place, but the old man snatched it out of his hands, taking a good deal of Edward's blistered palm with it.

The pain was almost enough to make Edward brave. The old man glared, challenging him to say or do something.

I'm almost seventeen, Edward thought. *Surely I'm as quick and as strong as this old man.*

But experience so far had proved otherwise. Apparently casual cruelty bred strength. Edward lowered his gaze and shuffled off to tend the animals, while the old man climbed onto the roof and set about fixing whatever it was he saw that Edward had done wrong in the thatching.

Come spring, Edward told himself. *Let him try me again, come spring.*

Edward fed the animals and then rounded them up and brought them into the cottage. The animals didn't seem to approve of this plan any more than Edward did. "All Hallows' Eve," Edward told them. "The witches'll get you." The animals didn't look convinced, and they scattered and balked and stepped on his toes with feet that were harder and heavier than they had any right to be. Some folk didn't believe in witches, but Edward knew they were real. Edward had reason to fear witches.

Finally all of the animals were indoors and the old man was satisfied with the thatching. Edward thought that at last the day's chores were done, but then the old man handed him the bucket to bring in water from the rain barrel, even though Edward had already fetched some earlier. Apparently not enough.

Not too many more days and there would be a film of ice on this water, Edward thought. Summer was hard, with the work of pulling the plow by hand, since the old man didn't have an ox, and the sweat running into his eyes, and the insects constantly biting. But hard as summer was, winter would be much, much worse, with the numbing cold, with the food dwindling—just him and the old man and the tiny cottage.

Edward brought the bucket to the door, which the old man had closed, another petty annoyance, as Edward needed both his sore hands to carry the bucket. He tried to shoulder the door open, but it appeared to be stuck. He kicked the door to get the old man's attention—the cottage was one room, so it wasn't like he could get lost in there. But the old man didn't come to let him in. Edward had to set the bucket down on the ground, causing twinges in both his back and his hands. He tried the door again, but it wouldn't budge.

"Hey!" he yelled. Had the old man lost his wits and placed the beam into the latch, forgetting that he'd sent Edward outside?

But still the old man didn't come to the door, and Edward remembered the look that had passed between them. Come spring, he had told himself, he'd have the strength to keep the old man from bullying him and from taking his petty rages out on him. The old man had realized this, too. Realized he had gotten all the compliant work he could out of Edward and now had locked him out. On All Hallows' Eve. The witches' sabbat.

"Let me in!" Edward shouted.

Smoke was coming from the chimney hole, and Edward could smell the soup they'd had at midday being reheated. It was mostly turnips, but there'd been a carrot, too. Edward had grown fond of treats like carrots this past year.

"Let me in for tonight," Edward called to the old man. "If you want me to leave tomorrow, I will."

He remembered the townsman with the stump for a hand. Useless as the old man always called Edward, at least during the summer there were tasks Edward could do. He didn't know why the old man and the old woman had taken him in, this time last year, except for anticipating his help during the course of the spring and summer months. Would he ever be able to find another couple, another soul to take him in just as autumn faded?

Edward flung the bucket of water against the door. He drew a mental picture of the water freezing overnight and the old man stepping on the ice in the morning, slipping, and breaking his neck. But most likely it wouldn't get that cold tonight. Cold enough to suck all the life's warmth out of Edward's body, but not cold enough to freeze water.

Edward had to satisfy himself by hoping the old man would fall asleep before remembering to block the chimney hole, so that the witches would be able to fly in and get him.

Of course, witches that spiteful and resourceful would surely get Edward first.

Edward wondered where he should try to hide, where the witches wouldn't think of.

But then he thought of the coming winter, and of the beggars, and of the men who had been maimed for being thieves.

Edward knew he could not survive the winter on his own. But could he, perhaps, survive the witches?

The sky was growing dark, but Edward headed off into the woods. There was a place there, near where the old woman had gone to get herbs. She had pointed the clearing out to him and had warned, "Witches dance," and had shaken her head vigorously to him not to cross that area.

Edward's scalp had crawled that day when he had recognized the place—the place he had found himself after his one disastrous encounter with a witch.

Edward had hated the woods because of the clearing, but now he headed for it, thinking the witches were his only hope.

Would he see again the witch who had sent him here? Did she dwell in this land? Would she—or any of her sisters—take pity on him, a year later? He had certainly learned his lesson, and he hoped that would be enough to satisfy a witch.

Shivering, with his inadequate clothing and his half-empty belly, he told himself the worst thing the witches could do would be to ignore him.

In the woods, the darkness settled around him quickly. His breath condensed in the night air, and the branches, almost bare, creaked alarmingly overhead. He found the stream and followed it to the lightning-struck tree, and then, there was the clearing.

He hunkered down, wrapping his arms around himself for warmth, and he watched the sky for a sign of the witches coming to celebrate their sabbat. He would apologize, he would beg, he would promise anything if they would only send him home. For he had certainly learned his lesson and he was no longer the same boy he had been last year.

A shadow crossed the moon, and then another, and then another, and then a whole swarm of shadows—the witches, flying on broomsticks, approaching the clearing.

Edward stood to wait for them. And while he waited, he remembered . . .

It hadn't been this cold last year—and he had had a thick jacket—when he had oh-so-foolishly gone out with his friends. They had all thrown rolls of toilet paper into the trees and shrubbery of the neighbor they thought was just a crazy old lady, but Edward had gone up onto the porch of her house, to unscrew the lightbulb from the lamp by her door, and to crack an egg or two on the windowpanes. That was when, suddenly, she had opened the door, home after all.

"You malicious little toad," she had called him—and now that Edward knew what she was, he supposed he should consider himself lucky that she hadn't actually turned him into a toad.

His friends had all very quickly scattered into other people's backyards, leaving him to face her alone.

"Well," he had said by way of explanation, "you didn't answer your doorbell."

She had folded her arms across her chest and looked down her nose at him.

Still trying to make a joke of it, Edward had said, "Trick or treat."

And she had said those words that had condemned him to this world, "Oh, trick," she had said with a malicious smile. "I definitely believe you deserve a trick."

MY REAL MOTHER

My adoptive mother always told me, "Evelyn, your real mother loved you so much, she gave you away."

I can't remember being young enough that this made sense to me. I always thought it was like saying, "I love chocolate so much, I never eat any." Or, "I love the color pink so much, I never wear it." Or, "I love Brad Pitt so much, I never go to his movies."

What's weird is that in fact, the older I got, the more ways I thought to *make* it make sense. Maybe you love chocolate, but you've got diabetes so you can't eat it; you love pink, but it makes you—personally, because of your coloring—look pale and washed-out; you love Brad Pitt, but you realize that good as he is to look at, his acting is a disappointment, so you better stick to just drooling over pictures of him.

So I tried to figure out *how* my mother could love me so much she had to give me away.

Some thoughts:

1. My mother found out, while she was pregnant with me or shortly after my birth that she was dying, and she knew it would be better for me to be placed immediately with another family rather than staying with a mother who was slowly fading and growing too weak to pick me up or feed me.

For my mother's illness, picture Nicole Kidman in *Moulin Rouge,* progressively getting dark circles under her eyes and elegantly coughing her lungs out. Or Bette Davis in that old black-and-white movie *Dark Victory,* where she bravely continues to work in her garden, hiding from her loved ones that she has gone blind due to a brain tumor.

But I figured if my real mother was dead, my adoptive mother would have simply said so.

Besides, I wanted her alive. I wanted to meet her.

So forget that, and start all over again.

1. My mother was a princess whose wicked father, the king, took me away from her—like in those Hercules movies from the '50s that show up at 2:00 A.M. on TNT: Italian movies of Greek myths dubbed in English. Talk about multicultural. Mythology is a place where there are lots of babies that kings need to get rid of because of prophecies about the child growing up to overthrow the kingdom.

Okay, Okay, the princess mother was a rationalization from when I was really young. I soon realized that there are a lot more princesses in fairy tales and movies than in real life.

And that girls don't generally grow up to usurp thrones, anyway.

Besides, it's hard to believe a modern-day king could get away with something like that in this age of talk radio and *60 Minutes* and *The National Enquirer.*

2. As I got older, I came to realize that a girl does not have to be a princess for her father to pressure her into giving up her baby. My mother could have been involved in a romance in the manner of Romeo and Juliet. (The Franco Zeffirelli version, with Leonard Whiting and Olivia Hussey, thank you very much. It's hard to take Leonardo DiCaprio seriously unless he's going down with the Titanic.)

Anyway, I figured that, though in my case the young lovers survived—or at least my mother did—the families didn't approve. They refused to allow them to marry, enrolled him (if he *was* still alive) in one of those wilderness therapy programs for at-risk teens, and sent her to await the birth of the baby with out-of-state relatives in one of those spooky old houses way out in the country, with no neighbors and only intermittent electricity. Then they put me up for adoption while she was still groggy from childbirth.

This scenario, I figured, was a strong possibility.

3. Or maybe, even, I wasn't actually physically wrested out of my mother's arms. It could have been that she was dirt-poor, and—not having the support of her family, and being depressed and wishing the best for me—she gave me up so that I would have a better life than she'd had. Stella Dallas, but with a mother who was economically deprived, not rude and crude and trashy.

But a lot can change in fifteen years. Whether or not her financial situation had improved, my real mother no doubt often wondered what had happened to me and, I was sure, regretted the decision, which had been forced on her or which she'd had to make.

I've always liked to picture her—looking up from her embroidery, there at a leaded-glass window in her father's castle, or taking a moment from plowing a field on that gothic farm, or sitting on the fire escape of her tenement apartment—resting her chin on her fist and gazing out into the distance, as she tried to picture me. Like Maria in *West Side Story*.

All right, all right, Maria was daydreaming about meeting a boyfriend, not a daughter. But I just knew my mother had expressed very similar sentiments to me—okay, probably not musically, but she'd said it. Only I'd been too young to remember.

Okay, moving on from what I guessed to what I knew: my adoptive mother. When she adopted me as an infant, my adoptive mother was single, but with a lot of money, both from her parents and from her career in telecommunications. We'd visit New York to go to Broadway plays, and to museums, and to gallery openings, and she signed me up for youth-theater group—since I *love* the movies—and for pottery classes and horseback-riding lessons. We got along fine when she could always hand me off to nannies or au pairs whenever she'd had enough of me.

But two years ago, she got married. My new father had been married before, and he brought two little boys along with him: Judd and Bradley. You just *know* that a three-year-old named Judd and a five-year-old named Bradley are going to be trouble. A movie director would have a field day casting the parts to go with those names.

All of a sudden, *somebody* or other decided that my adoptive mother should be a stay-at-home mom to take care of all three of us while the new husband continued in *his* career. Although she agreed to this arrangement, in her heart my adoptive mother was cranky. And, as long as she was home, anyway, with all that newfound extra time on her hands and me just becoming a teen-ager, she decided it was time to embark on the Let's-Improve-Evelyn Program.

Suddenly, as far as she was concerned, I could do absolutely nothing right.

Suddenly, as far as *I* was concerned, she became the headmistress from *The Little Princess*.

The adoptive stepfather was a self-absorbed over-achiever, who would always say that he couldn't see things:

"Evelyn, I can't see what your problem is."

"Evelyn, I can't see why you can't just try to get along with Judd and Bradley."

"Evelyn, I can't see why you feel you have to take that tone with your mother."

And when I would correct him by telling him, "*Adoptive* mother," he'd say, "Evelyn, I can't see why you have to say that every single time."

Well, if he couldn't see it, there was no use my try-ing to explain.

Two years of that, and I decided it was time to find my real mother.

Thanks to the Internet—and to a sizable chunk of change in my bank account that accumulated during the absentee-adoptive-mother guilty-conscience phase—I was able to track her down.

I learned her name—Bonnie Ryan—and that her home was in Bainbridge, only a couple of hours' drive away from where I lived, in Corning. Her address had changed from the one on the adoption papers, but I was persistent, like Frances McDormand's character in *Fargo*. Except, I like to think, more attractive.

When I told my adoptive parents what I had learned, they couldn't see why I would want to meet her.

Well, *duh!* My plan wasn't just to *meet* her; I wanted to go back to live with her: Put the Parkhurst stage of my life behind me and reacquaint myself with my rightful Ryan heritage.

We had a *big* fight, my adoptive parents and me. They talked about her privacy, and about how those kinds of records are supposed to be sealed, and how—maybe—she had gone on to make a new life without me and that my showing up could complicate things for her in a bad way.

They also lectured me on the fact that life was not like in the movies.

Well, *duh!* again. I'd already figured that out on my own, with the whole princess thing.

I pointed out to my adoptive parents that the only reason I'd been able to find my real mother was because I'm so computer savvy. If she'd had the resources, *she* would have found *me*.

And apparently there was a Mr. Ryan. According to the adoption forms, my father was Marty Ryan; and my mother now lived with a Marty Ryan. So it wasn't like I was going to come as a big surprise to a husband who hadn't realized she'd had a child.

I figured I'd been right with scenario number one, the Romeo and Juliet romance that the manipulative families had tried to break up. But Bonnie and Marty, once they'd been old enough, had been able to get away from their families and find one another. All they needed to make their lives complete was to find me.

Except that I'd found them first.

Where was the problem there?

My adoptive parents got stubborn and downright mean.

I got stubborn and mean right back at them.

Long story short: I ended up needing a bandage on my arm, and I knew I had to get out of that house.

By coincidence, it was Halloween, but that just fit in extra well with my plan to visit my real mother that very night. My real *parents*: *That* thought would take some getting used to. Despite my adoptive parents' objections. I decided I would go in disguise, to ease my way in. Sort of like trick *and* treat.

My adoptive parents had bought tickets to some sort of Halloween extravaganza party at one of the big hotels downtown, so Judd and Bradley were spending the whole weekend at their mother's, for a change, and weren't due back till Monday after school—which was cause for celebration in and of itself.

I went into my adoptive mother's closet and got this sparkly silver evening dress that she'd worn back in her sophisticated corporate-entertainment days. From my youth-theater-group days, I found a rhinestone tiara that I'd worn in our production of *Cinderella*.

I put touches of J. Lo's Glow on my pulse points for luck, because she played a Cinderella-type character in *Maid in Manhattan*. Then, standing in front of the full-length mirror, I said out loud, "Who says there aren't fairy tale princesses anymore?"

So that my real mother would see that I was a trick-or-treater on her doorstep, and not the elegant woman I appeared to be, I took Bradley's hollow plastic pumpkin that he'd left behind in the whirlwind of his mother picking him up Friday night.

Planning ahead, I got out the big plastic Halloween bowl and the bags of candy my adoptive mother had bought. Since there would be nobody home to answer our bell once it got late enough for the trick-or-treating to begin, I set the bowlful of candy down on a wooden TV tray on the porch by the front door. That wouldn't last long, once kids realized no one was home, but there wasn't much else I could do—unless I waited for the trick-or-treating to be over. And that would have me arriving at my real parents' house in Bainbridge incredibly late, since it was over two hours away from Corning.

Two hours by car.

Driving was yet another of those things my adoptive parents and I had frequently quarreled about. Yes, technically speaking, I wasn't old enough for my driver's permit. But a lot of my friends were getting lessons from their parents or older siblings, at least in parking lots and on back roads. To give them a head start once they turned sixteen. Planning ahead. I liked to plan ahead. My adoptive parents said I had to wait.

Luckily, they were totally oblivious to the fact that my boyfriend, Robert—who's eighteen even though I've told them sixteen—has let me practice in his car.

My adoptive mother's car keys were in a little crystal bowl on her dresser. All I needed was to drive slowly and carefully—the way I always do—and pretend Robert was sitting beside me to give advice if I needed it. Which I wouldn't.

No time for dinner, so I grabbed a candy bar from the trick-or-treat bowl on the porch. The Mr. and Mrs. Scarecrow figures were slumped on either side of the door, Mr. Scarecrow holding a pumpkin, Mrs. Scarecrow wearing a witch hat. I'd painted smiles on their burlap-bag faces, figuring *someone* in this house needed to be happy. Going down the front stairs to begin my new life with my real mother, I felt as poised and classy and glamorous as Grace Kelly, who was an actress *and* a princess.

Things went downhill from there.

The car kind of scraped a bit against the doorway of the garage as I backed out. I planned never to return, and it was truly a tiny scratch, and I figured my adoptive mother would never see it, so there was nothing to worry about. But still . . .

Then, once I was on the road, when I bit into the candy bar, a flake of chocolate dropped off and fell onto the silver dress right between my breasts, leaving a little spot of brown, which—when I tried to rub it away— became a little smear of brown.

I stopped at a gas station mini-mart to wash up, but the attendant said there was no public restroom. So I bought some bottled water and poured a bit of that onto the dress, which made the little brown smear spread into definitely medium-sized proportions, smack in the middle of a damp spot that could only be labeled as *big*.

The mini-mart attendant sold me some hand soap in a pump dispenser, and now the damp brown smear took on the added quality of foaminess.

I poured more water until the brown finally faded.

Now, however, the damp area extended alarmingly, and the fabric—where I'd been scrubbing at it—was stretched out right in that most obvious of places.

Corning, where I'd said good-bye forever to my old home, was a good twenty minutes back down the road I'd just driven, plus I'd already spent another twenty minutes in the mini-mart—which meant that if I wanted to go back and change, I'd have lost a whole hour. That's without even taking into consideration that I'd already settled on this outfit as being perfect and I'd have to figure out what else I could wear.

I looked at the bandage on my arm—a memento from my adoptive family, the last mark they would leave on me. I could not go back.

And there was something else I'd forgotten to take into consideration when I'd been planning this out—how early it gets dark this time of year.

Even Robert never let me drive in the dark.

It was too late to change my mind—either about the plan as a whole, or about my outfit. I told myself confidently that I would just have to count on the fabric drying in the hour and a half that it would take me to drive the rest of the way to my real parents' house.

The driving instructions, which had seemed so clear when I'd gotten them off the Internet, were *not* clear, at least not for me, not in the dark, anxious and nervous as I was and sweating so much that the scent of all that Glow was making me dizzy. I had to open the window, which made the car cold, so I had to turn on the heater, whose noise got on my nerves.

The computer's estimate for driving time had been two hours, seven minutes. In my planning, I'd rounded that up to two hours, fifteen minutes, so that I'd assumed I'd be ringing the doorbell at my real mother's house sometime around a quarter to seven.

At twenty after nine, I pulled into the driveway of what I hoped was the right house. It was hard to be certain, since people in this neighborhood didn't seem to believe in fricking house numbers. Pumpkins, yes. Orange lights, plenty of them. But numbers? I was looking for 1593, and had passed a house whose mailbox was painted with what may have been 1509 or 1569, then there were a whole bunch of houses that didn't seem to have any number on them at all, until one where the number over the garage was 1615.

Despite cruising down that street four times, I couldn't make out any more numbers, nor did the numbers go up in any reasonable way—like by twos, fives or tens—to let me count off.

Isn't there some sort of law that house numbers have to be visible from the street?

But across the street from this house was one that had the words *fifteen ninety-six,* in script, over their garage door. (Try reading *that* while driving a car—the first time you've driven alone or for longer than fifteen minutes—down a dark, unfamiliar street when you're pissed off at just about everything the day has thrown at you already.) The house I was looking for had to be this one or the one next door. This one still had lots of lights on, which made it look more inviting. Lights, despite the late hour. And despite the fact that all the trick-or-treaters must either be asleep by now or bouncing off the walls of their own bedrooms due to sugar highs.

My heart was beating so hard I wondered if I had found my real mother just in time to die in her arms of a ruptured aorta. Writer Charlie Kaufman goes in for that kind of irony in his films.

I got out of the car, and finally saw the number, 1593, written vertically on the post next to the front door. It *was* the right house.

Nice neighborhood, in spite of the lack of numbers. Nice house. Big house.

I took several deep breaths, but nothing was getting my heart rate settled into anything near normal. I rested the trick-or-treat pumpkin into the crook of my elbow à la Dorothy with her basket on the road to the Emerald City. Then, restraining myself from glancing down to check how the bodice of my dress had dried, I walked up to the front door.

The bell chimed a snatch of a classical tune that sounded familiar, from the sound track of some movie or another, but I couldn't place it.

The door opened.

I'd been afraid that my real mother—not immediately recognizing that it was me—might be irritated to have someone show up so late on her doorstep on Halloween night.

But standing there in the doorway were two people who were obviously very into Halloween. It was a woman and a man, and they were dressed like rag dolls, like Raggedy Ann and Raggedy Andy. It made me think, just for a moment, of the Mr. and Mrs. Scarecrow figures on the porch of the house that used to be mine. The house I would never go back to. Though there was no reason for it to, not now, my arm under the bandage began to ache anew.

Far from sounding put out by my late arrival, Raggedy Andy chanted: "Trick or treat, smell my feet, gimme something good to eat."

"No, Andy," Raggedy Ann told him. Bonnie. Bonnie Ryan. My real mother. I immediately liked her voice. Kind of smoky like Lauren Bacall's, but friendly, too, like Julia Roberts. Obviously part of a spiel they'd worked out, she said, "*We* give *them* something good to eat."

Clearly Raggedy Andy—Marty Ryan—knew that, because he was holding a big black bowl full of candy. But he asked, in the simple way you'd expect from a person with rags in his head, "And do we smell *their* feet?"

"No, Andy," my mother told him firmly. "Nobody smells anybody's feet."

He bowed, holding out the candy bowl, which was probably more necessary for the average-sized trick-or-treater than for someone of my age and height.

Despite that extra two and a half hours in the car, I hadn't come up with just the right entrance line. "Um...," I said.

Marty cocked his head, like androids always seem to in sci-fi films, to show he was concentrating so as not to miss anything.

My mother smiled graciously. With all of their theatrical makeup, it was hard to tell what they *really* looked like. But they had kind eyes. And I knew she was beautiful, and he was handsome.

"Are you all right?" my mother asked, and suddenly the playfulness was gone from her voice. She sounded concerned, not impatient to get me off her front stoop.

"Yes," I managed to squeak.

"Your heart's beating so fast," she said.

"You can *hear* it?" Maybe it *was* about to explode.

Gently, she rested a fingertip at my throat, and I realized she could see the blood pulsing through my veins. My mother was as observant as she was kind. I wondered if she was a doctor or a nurse.

Marty was still in his Raggedy Andy persona. "Maybe we should invite her in?" he suggested, acting as though he was having trouble holding his head up straight. "I sometimes get wobbly when I stand too long."

"Marty," my mother chided him, letting him know this was not playing, and she took my arm and led me into the living room.

From outside, it had looked like a nice house in a nice neighborhood, but inside was very impressive. It looked like the kind of house that ends up as a six- or eight-page spread in a magazine about elegant homes. Marty and Bonnie had done quite well for themselves in the years since they'd had to give me up because they couldn't afford a good home in which to raise me.

Bonnie had me sit down on the couch, and she sat next to me.

I was sitting next to my real mother.

"Marty, why don't you get the poor child a glass of

water?" she said. "And turn off the front light. I don't think there are going to be any more trick-or-treaters tonight."

Child? I was disappointed. "Oh, dear," I said. "I hoped to look like an adult princess." My first sentence to my real mother.

"Well," Bonnie said, trying hard to please, "a *young* adult princess."

I appreciated the effort.

Marty sat down on the other side of me and handed me a frosty glass of water, complete with ice cubes. Very thoughtful.

I sipped at the water.

"So . . . ," Marty said, friendly but inquisitive, the Raggedy Andy muddleheadedness gone entirely. "May we ask who, exactly, you are?"

"Evelyn Parkhurst."

No reaction at all.

Which made sense. The adoption agency wouldn't have given them the name of the woman who adopted me.

"Evelyn," I repeated. The papers just said "baby girl," but I thought it could have been that my mother had suggested the name to the social worker or the person in charge; she could have said, "That's what I've been calling my dear baby that I have to give up for her own good, and maybe you could ask her new, rich mother to call her that."

But apparently not.

"You drove here," Marty said, which meant they'd heard the car—either that or he'd seen it in the driveway when he'd gone to the kitchen to get the water. He continued, "Most of our trick-or-treaters don't come by car."

"I imagine not," I said. I was about to say it—*I'm your daughter*—when he kept on talking, asking, "So where are you from?"

"Corning."

His eyebrows—both the yarn-colored painted-on ones and the real ones—went up, and he glanced at his wife. They both moved in a bit closer to me as though they could tell I needed comforting, and she put her arm around my shoulders—a very friendly gesture.

Again I was about to tell them, when he asked, "Lost?"

"No," I admitted. "Looking for you specifically."

Neither of them appeared as surprised as I would have thought.

"I think," I said—I was sure, but needed a running start before I could get it out—"I think I'm your daughter."

"Really?" my mother asked.

I was a bit disconcerted how evenly she said that: not surprised; neither pleased nor distressed.

"And how did you find us?" Marty asked.

"Internet." Somehow, though he had moved no closer, my perception of his closeness veered abruptly from making me feel comfortable to making me feel uneasy. I was aware of my stepbrother Bradley's plastic pumpkin, which was still looped over my arm, pressing into my side. I shifted myself away from my father, closer to my mother.

"Did you tell anyone you were coming here?" my mother asked.

"No," I said, a moment before I realized her arm had me pretty much blocked in.

"One way to be sure . . . ," Marty murmured, leaning toward me.

The next thing I knew, he had put his hands on my thighs, pressing me down into the couch so that I could not get up. And my mother—my real mother—grabbed my shoulders, then sank her teeth into my neck.

My mother was drinking my blood.

There must have been something in my mother's saliva, some anti-panic enzyme, to keep me from struggling—either that or she exerted some sort of mind control. I knew she was a vampire. I mean, come on!—she was sucking blood out of my neck. But the

horror was more on an intellectual level than the stom-
ach-churning, frantic, I'm-about-to-die terror that it
should have been. At the same time, it wasn't that my
mind had shut down, because I was aware of the tick-
ing of the clock on the mantel. I had dropped—all
unaware—the glass of water Marty had brought for
me, but now I could feel that cold wet spot on my hip.
I could also feel the fabric of the couch scratching the
backs of my thighs, and I could see the strands of yarn
that formed the curls of my mother's Raggedy Ann
wig. I could smell the thick stage makeup she wore,
and I could smell my own blood.

Was I about to die, or were my parents going to
make me into one of the undead to join them forever?
I wasn't sure what to hope for.

My mother shoved me away from her and spat my
blood out onto that expensive hardwood floor. She
made a disgusted, boy-have-I-bitten-into-something-
bad sound to go along with her boy-have-I-bitten-
into-something-bad expression.

"She's right," my mother told her husband, "she
has our blood in her veins. But with the human gene,
not the vampire."

"Drat!" Marty said. "One of our worthless off-
spring coming back like a bad penny. I was hoping she
was wrong entirely and we could have her."

One of?

Worthless?

"Well, the night's still young," my mother consoled him. "We'll find *someone*." My real parents were disappointed that they had to go out rather than have home delivery.

She hauled me up off the couch and started dragging me toward the front door. "So nice of you to come to visit," she said. "Now scram."

"But . . . ," I said. "But . . . but . . ."

"We didn't want you—which one are you?—fifteen years ago. We don't want you now. We can't raise you as a vampire; we can't feed on you. You're totally useless. Go back to where you came from."

"But . . . ," I said again.

She closed the door in my face.

"But . . ."

I stood on their front step like an idiot, thinking I couldn't go back to Corning. My arm throbbed. Considering the mess I'd left, there was *no way* I could go back.

But my choices had gotten dramatically fewer.

In the end, I suppose I was lucky. They could have killed me, even if my blood was no good to them—just to make sure I didn't turn them in. Maybe they knew nobody would believe me. Maybe they changed their identities periodically. They must, at least once every twenty years or so, being creatures that never aged or died. Even if I *did* get someone to believe me and go there with me, my vampire parents would have moved on.

Hard to say, because I couldn't see how telling about them would help me.

It took me even longer to drive back to Corning because I still couldn't understand the map directions, *plus* I was so upset with all that had happened that I kept losing track of what I was doing.

So it was four o'clock in the morning when I pulled into the driveway of my adoptive parents' house. Another hour before the easternmost edge of the sky would be turning pink.

I didn't even try to put the car back in the garage.

The pumpkin was smashed on the front walk, the TV tray was upside down in the bushes, and the plastic bowl—empty, of course—had been tossed onto the garage roof.

So much for hoping for civilized trick-or-treaters.

I sat down between Mr. and Mrs. Scarecrow, leaning against the front door so that I felt the coolness of it through the fabric of my adoptive mother's party dress. I didn't want to go in, face that mess in the living room, all that blood, including a bit of my own.

I touched the bandage on my arm, where I'd used the knife on myself to get blood to leave a handprint, as though, wounded, I'd tried to get to the phone. So I'd look—even though I was missing—like another victim, an abductee.

"Well," I said to Mr. and Mrs. Scarecrow's burlap-covered faces, "you were wrong about life not being like the movies. This evening has been very much à la Alfred Hitchcock."

Luckily, no one had messed with them. Or not badly, anyway.

I'm guessing, by their slightly altered positions, by the way they were doubled over, that someone had given them a kick or two. Whoever had done that hadn't carried on, for whatever reason. Perhaps from a slightly skittish feeling that *something* was amiss, a feeling too vague—or too real—to investigate.

Or maybe Mr. and Mrs. Scarecrow's positions had shifted when the rigor mortis set in.

I readjusted the hat on my adoptive mother's head. It had seemed such a good plan this afternoon.

HOLDING ON

Harlan is playing with the cat when the cat suddenly focuses its attention on a spot somewhere behind Harlan's left shoulder. Harlan feels a sudden chill, as though he had been sitting cross-legged in front of a refrigerator whose door someone opened.

Harlan tries to tell himself that the steady gaze at something no human can see is in the nature of cats. He has just articulated this explanation to himself when the cat bristles its fur, arches its back, and hisses.

At the same moment, Harlan catches the whiff of smoke.

It must be Halloween again, Harlan thinks.

He stands and turns.

He can see through the boy, a boy whom Harlan estimates to be about fifteen or sixteen. Harlan has been seeing the boy for what must be eight years now, and in that passing of years, they are finally the same age.

Harlan wonders if this is significant in the interaction of ghosts with the living.

As has happened before, but only on Halloween nights, Harlan can make out not only the boy, but some of his surroundings—as though, on this one night of the year, the fabric that separates the living from the dead grows thin enough to see through.

It is night, and the boy is in a room whose ceiling has caved in and is open to the sky. There is broken furniture and debris, great gaping holes in the walls, and stains of both fire and water—evidence that the firefighters came, though obviously not soon enough.

Harlan very much doubts that this room exists anymore, in either world. It is more a state of mind.

The boy is sitting cross-legged in a space in the rubble, a position very similar to how Harlan had just been sitting, but without the cat.

The cat, fickle friend, has abandoned Harlan to face on his own whatever is coming.

"Helloooo," Harlan calls, trying to sound friendly.

Sometimes the boy seems able to hear him, sometimes not.

Harlan can never hear the boy.

The boy shivers, which may or may not mean that he has heard Harlan.

There are dark circles under the boy's eyes, and he rocks back and forth, his arms tight around himself as though his stomach hurts.

Harlan wishes there were something he could do to ease the boy's pain, but there is not.

"It's all right," Harlan tells him. "Don't be afraid."

Harlan knows he has no idea what he is talking about. Things may or may not be all right in the boy's world. For all Harlan knows, the boy may have every reason to be afraid.

During previous visits, not much more than this has ever happened:

- Harlan sees the boy.
- The boy is in distress.
- Eventually the boy fades away.

Sometimes the boy has broken down and cried, great wracking sobs, more heartbreaking for the fact that Harlan cannot hear the slightest whimper. Once, the boy had picked up one of the pieces of charred wood, a section of ceiling beam or wall brace—thick, but no more than a foot or so long. To Harlan's horror the boy had smacked the wood against his own forehead, repeatedly.

"Stop!" Harlan had shouted at him. "Don't do that!"

He didn't think the boy had heard him.

The boy had stopped, finally, worn out, blood streaming down his face. Then he had curled himself up into a tight ball and stayed that way, unmoving, until his image had faded away.

Now, there's a fevered look in the boy's eyes that reminds Harlan of that day, and he hopes not to see that awful scene reenacted.

The boy reaches behind himself.

Harlan is cringing, but it isn't a piece of board the boy brings forward; it's a backpack.

A backpack is such an ordinary thing that for one moment Harlan dares to believe all is well.

The boy opens the pack and takes out a rope.

There is no instant of confusion or doubt for Harlan. No search for an alternative explanation. Though he's never seen this before, Harlan knows what the boy plans to do with that rope.

"Stop!" Harlan shouts at him. "There's no reason to end your life!"

The boy flings one end of the rope around a beam, which extends jaggedly partway across the ceiling, and secures that end; then he makes a noose of the other end. He finds what's left of a chair. The red plastic seat has partly melted, then solidified, but the boy is able to stand up on it. He passes the noose over his head and around his neck.

Harlan knows there is a heaven, but he doesn't

want to see the boy take that step. "Stop, stop, stop, stop!" he yells.

He suspects the boy might hear a whisper of this, for the boy claps his hands over his ears.

Then he steps off the chair.

The rope goes taut.

The boy's arms instinctively jerk out as though to break his fall.

And he does fall—but it's all the way to the floor, because the beam has broken beneath his weight.

The boy crumples in a heap, the rope landing around him, the piece of beam the other end is fastened to smacking him on the back of the head.

For a moment, as the boy lies motionless, Harlan wonders if he *has* succeeded in killing himself—except by blunt-force trauma rather than by hanging.

But apparently he has just had the wind knocked out of him. He stirs. He raises his hand to where the chunk of wood struck his head. He moans.

He moans, and Harlan can hear.

For the first time in eight years, Harlan can hear the boy.

He doesn't know if it's that synchronicity, after all this time, of their ages, or if it has something to do with the boy almost—though not quite—dying.

But Harlan steps forward and suddenly finds himself going through that barrier of cold that separates their worlds, and into that room with the singed and water-damaged wallpaper that hangs in dusty, smoky sheets.

He kneels beside the boy. His hand passes through him, but Harlan feels something—like a slight electric tingle.

The boy whips around on the floor and looks at Harlan in terror. Even though he was about to take his own life, now he's afraid, and he cringes and backs away from Harlan.

Harlan can hear his slight gasp. He can hear the scrape across the wooden floor of one of the metal studs on the boy's jeans pocket.

Since the rules appear to have changed, Harlan says, "I don't mean you any harm."

The boy goes to wrap his arms around himself, and feels the rope. He looks down at the rope, then at Harlan, then he looks up at what's left of the broken beam by the ceiling. Then back at Harlan.

"I know who you are." The boy's voice is a whisper, but clear.

Harlan says, "Fine. I know who you are."

The boy reacts as though Harlan has slapped him. He puts his face in his hands—as Harlan remembers, again, that time the boy sat here rocking and hitting himself in the face. Harlan realizes he's seen, without noting, lines—scars—on the boy's forehead.

"I'm sorry," the boy says. "I'm sorry, I'm sorry, I'm sorry . . ."

He keeps on repeating this until Harlan can take it no longer. He puts his hand out. If they were two living people, he would be resting his hand on the boy's shoulder. It's a sensation like trying to hold on to a handful of water.

"It was an accident," Harlan says.

"It was an accident," the boy agrees.

Harlan says, "You didn't mean it," at the exact moment the boy blurts out, "I didn't mean it."

The boy says, "I only wanted a glowing jack-o'-lantern, like I'd seen in pictures. Not just a hollowed-out pumpkin."

Harlan says, "I understand."

The boy says, "My fault, my fault, my fault." But he lets go of that thought before Harlan has to intervene again, and continues, "My mother said a candle was too dangerous for a seven-year-old to play with, but I never wanted to play with it; I just wanted to make the pumpkin glow. I took a candle from the dining room table, and her lighter, and after she'd tucked me in, I got up again and set the candle in the pumpkin and lit it, and it looked just like I hoped it would. Then . . . then . . ."

Harlan knows what the "then" is, but waits for the boy.

"Stupid," the boy says, "stupid, stupid, stupid, stupid, stupid. The candle was too tall, and the pumpkin lid wouldn't fit on, and the curtain touched the flame— just the tiniest edge of it—and the next thing I knew, the curtains were on fire and there was this awful loud alarm, and there was smoke everywhere, and my mother was picking me up and carrying me out of the apartment." He looks at Harlan with eyes of wonder and horror. "We didn't know you were home in the upstairs apartment. Your parents' car wasn't in the driveway, and we thought you were with them."

Once more, the boy starts repeating, "Stupid, stupid . . ."

Harlan interrupts him, saying, "I don't hold this against you."

The boy doesn't believe him. The boy says, "You keep coming back."

Harlan corrects him: "You keep calling me back."

The boy thinks this over. The image of the burned room quivers, like a heat mirage, as the boy loosens his hold on it. He asks, "You don't hate me?"

Through the moonlit, burned bedroom, Harlan can make out another room—a basement. This is the room the boy is really in; the bedroom, the room where Harlan died, is only a memory. Harlan sees that what the boy's rope has really pulled down is not a burned beam, but one of the furnace's heat runs. There *is* a ceiling, but no wallpaper, no charred remains.

"Live a good life," Harlan advises him.

Sometime during this brief exchange, the cat has come back, and Harlan scoops it up and carries it back where it belongs.

Where they both belong.

"Lead a good life," Harlan repeats to the boy, and never looks back.

Vivian Vande Velde is the celebrated author of more than twenty books for teen and middle grade readers, including *Three Good Deeds*, *Heir Apparent*, *Wizard at Work*, the short-story collection *Being Dead*, and the Edgar Award–winning *Never Trust a Dead Man*. She lives in Rochester, New York.

To learn more about Ms. Vande Velde and her books, visit **www.vivianvandevelde.com**.

More books you may enjoy . . . if you dare

ODDEST OF ALL
By Bruce Coville

"By turns creepy, funny, and thought-provoking, these atmospheric tales run the gamut from mystery and sci-fi to fantasy and horror."—*Horn Book*

BLUE MOON
By Hila Feil

"All the classic gothic conventions are here: the outsider-heroine's narrative, a mysterious death, a dark male stranger, a sage family friend, and natural phenomena galore of sea, storms, and fog."—*The Bulletin*

LOOK FOR ME BY MOONLIGHT
By Mary Downing Hahn

"A deliciously spine-tingling story."
—*Publishers Weekly*

A DEADLY GAME OF MAGIC
By Joan Lowery Nixon

"Nixon keeps the suspense cooking on all burners . . . an original, heart-pounding thriller."—*SLJ*

THE SÉANCE
By Joan Lowery Nixon

Winner of the Edgar Allan Poe Award for
Best Young Adult Mystery
"Real can't-stop-till-I-know-who-done-it
reading."—*SLJ*

THE SHE
By Carol Plum-Ucci

"Grippingly suspenseful."—*Kirkus Reviews*

BLACKTHORN WINTER
By Kathryn Reiss

"Mystery fans will enjoy this well-plotted
story, which [combines] budding romance,
family problems, amnesia, international travel
and murder."—*Kirkus Reviews*

DREADFUL SORRY
By Kathryn Reiss

"Spooky and satisfying."—*The Bulletin*